AMELIA'S TOUCH

ELIZABETH KELLY

EK PUBLISHING INC.

AMELIA'S TOUCH

She craves his touch.

Amelia Barlow is cursed.

After waking from a car accident at sixteen that killed her twin brother, she could hear other people's thoughts simply by touching them.

Unable to live a normal life, she retreats from society and resigns to a life alone.

However, a chance meeting with handsome detective Jack Emerson changes everything.

Targeted by an unstable Lycan, Amelia must rely on Jack to keep her safe. As it turns out, touching him isn't what she expected, leaving her craving for more.

Detective Jack Emerson is half-Lycan and half-human. His vampire hunt leads him to Amelia's hometown. He is immediately drawn to the sweet, innocent Amelia and finds her refusal to touch him puzzling.

Until he discovers her secret.

Jack's discovery that he may be the only person who can

keep Amelia from living a lonely life rattles him. As does his overpowering attraction to her.

Their mutual attraction is the least of their problems - the Lycans want her power, and they'll destroy everything to get it.

* * *

CHAPTER 1

I t was always the same. The same stretch of highway, the same mid-afternoon thunderstorm. The windshield wipers sweeping furiously across the glass did little to improve the visibility against the pouring rain. Her hands gripped the steering wheel so tightly that her knuckles were white.

Slowly, the tendons in her neck creaking, she turned her head to the passenger's side, praying that, just once, the dream would be different. It wasn't. There was Richard, her sweet, tender-hearted Richard. He was squinting through the glass, and while her heart began a jittery, rapid beating in her chest - knowing the horrific path this dream was about to take - she couldn't stop the rush of love at seeing him again.

Although it hurt, hurt plenty, in fact, to stare at his strong jaw, the patch of hair on his face that he insisted was a beard and the thick dark hair that covered his head, it was a bitter-sweet pain. Her dreams were the only place she saw him now. Even as she prepared herself for the horror that was to come, she couldn't stop staring at him, soaking in every detail from the small razor cut on his throat to the missing button on his shirt.

He turned to her, his tanned face uncharacteristically pale. "Something's not right. I think you should pull over."

In reality, she'd laughed and chided him gently, reaching out with one hand to punch his shoulder and tease him about being a worrywart. In her dreams, she said nothing – just continued driving toward the small hill. She wanted to scream at him and beg him to make her pull the car over right now - there was nothing but pain and death at the top of that hill - but she was paralyzed in her seat. She could only watch helplessly as they crested the hill.

The dream unfolded in dismayingly slow motion. The horrifying moment of terror as the old pick-up truck veered into their lane. Richard's panicked shout as he reached over and pushed the steering wheel, turning his side into the path of the oncoming truck. She felt the crushing agony in her leg as their small car collided with the truck. The loud screaming of metal against metal deafened her, and tiny shards of glass embedded into her skin as the windshield shattered and the rain rushed in. The bright burst of pain as something heavy and hard struck her directly above her temple.

As the darkness closed around her, she looked one final time at Richard. His warm and expressive eyes were now empty and cold. A steady stream of blood flowed from the top of his head and over the bridge of his nose. The darkness was all around her now, but she opened her mouth and shrieked before it completely consumed her. Her Richard was lost to her forever, and she screamed and screamed and –

Amelia jolted awake. She was sweating and shaking, and the room had a high-pitched keening noise. After a moment, she realized the noise was coming from her. She sat up on the couch, wrapping her arms around her trembling legs. She forced herself to concentrate on her breathing - long, flat inhales through her nose followed by slow, steady exhales out of her mouth. Remnants of her nightmare still clung to her like an old overcoat, but years of self-soothing had made her a pro at it, and when the shrill ring of her cell phone interrupted the late afternoon quiet, she barely flinched.

She reached for the phone, glanced at the number and sighed. "Hello, Ray."

"Hello, Amelia." Ray's voice was always so somber when he talked to her. Made sense, considering he only called her when it was particularly bad.

"Can you come in? We need your help." He paused. "It would be best if you hurried."

Amelia's hand automatically went to the small scar visible at her hairline, her fingers rubbing over her raised skin. "I can be there in half an hour."

* * *

"I'M REAL SORRY ABOUT THE WAIT, DETECTIVE EMERSON." The sheriff's receptionist, he thought she had said her name was Susan, handed him a Styrofoam cup of foul-looking coffee and sat down beside him.

"Don't trouble yourself, Susan." Jack grinned at her and watched with amusement as she flushed. She had to be at least fifty-five, but it was good to know his smile could still affect the fifty and above crowd.

He sipped tentatively at the coffee. It tasted better than it looked, thank God. "It seems like there's a lot of activity happening this evening for such a small town."

Based on his research, the sheriff's office employed two full-time deputies and three part-time deputies. All five

3

deputies were currently in the office, nearly tripping over each other in the small space.

Susan leaned closer. "Truth be told, we normally don't have much going on here, but Julie – she's a clerk at the Sip 'N Save - and her daughter have been missing for two days. Sheriff Dunmore thinks her husband Ed has something to do with it."

She paused and lowered her voice. "Ed has a temper and a drinking problem, and he was real upset when Julie took the baby and left him a few months ago."

She shifted in the hard plastic chair. "Ed himself has been missing for a few days. When he showed up tonight at Julie's mama's house demanding to speak to Julie, Louise – that's Julie's mama - called Sheriff Dunmore right away."

She stood. "Anyway, Sheriff wanted to question Ed immediately, which is why you're having a bit of a wait. He didn't forget about your appointment, Detective Emerson."

"Call me Jack."

Susan flushed again. "Jack, then. And forgive me, but is that an actual wolf?" She pointed to the large animal lying motionless at Jack's feet.

"He's a hybrid, actually."

"He looks just like a wolf." Susan stared at the beast with more than a touch of apprehension, but the dog completely ignored her.

"Yeah, he gets that a lot." Jack nudged the dog with his foot, and he sat up so that Jack could scratch the top of his head. His tongue lolled out of his mouth, and he grinned happily.

Susan stepped back. "Well, the sheriff shouldn't be too much longer."

The phone rang, and she returned to her seat behind the front desk.

The bell over the door chimed, and Jack glanced up at the

tall, curvy brunette entering the office. The dog at his feet sniffed the air delicately, and Jack's nostrils flared as a deliciously intoxicating scent of vanilla and jasmine filled the office. The dog leaned forward eagerly, half-rising on his haunches, but Jack touched his shoulder, and the dog quieted.

Jack stared at the woman as she walked toward the front desk. She wore a long, blue cotton skirt and paired the skirt with a plain white t-shirt. Oddly, she wore a pair of white evening gloves. The gloves covered her skin to the middle of her biceps. Her dark brown hair hung nearly to her waist in a carefully made braid.

His eyes dropped to her ass. The skirt hugged it like a second skin, and he wondered idly if she was wearing a thong. The lack of panty lines suggested she was.

Still on the phone, Susan smiled at the woman and raised her hand in a 'give me a minute' gesture. The woman nodded and moved to the bank of chairs where Jack sat patiently. She paused before choosing a seat, leaving an empty chair between them.

The dog sat up straight. He stared eagerly at the woman, and Jack watched as he sniffed at the air repeatedly. He shifted in the woman's direction, and Jack placed his hand again on the dog's shoulder. This time, the dog ignored him. A low whine started in his throat, and he pulled free of Jack's hand and moved toward the woman, yipping excitedly. She gasped when the dog placed his head in her lap. He stared up at her, whining eagerly as his tail wagged furiously.

Shocked by his dog's behaviour, Jack took a few seconds to give his usual spiel. "He's not a wolf. He's a hybrid. And he's gentle."

The woman didn't look like the panicking type, but the last thing he needed was a hysterical woman on his hands. She smiled at the dog and brushed one gloved hand across the top of his head. She glanced up at him, and he was fascinated by her clear ocean blue eyes.

"What's his name?" Her voice was low with an almost musical lilt to it.

"Lupe." He cleared his throat.

She cocked her head to the side for a moment. "Clever."

She stripped off first one glove, then the other and placed them on the empty seat between them. She paused and then, tentatively, like she was expecting a shock, ran the tips of her fingers over the soft fur on the side of Lupe's neck. She closed her eyes for a moment. A shiver ran through her body, and he could see goosebumps popping up on her skin. She sighed and buried both hands deep into the fur. She opened her eyes and smiled at Lupe, who stared back at her rapturously.

"Ooh, him's a good boy, isn't him? Such a good puppy he is." She spoke in a coddling baby voice as she scratched his neck and shoulders, and Jack watched in amazement as the dog tried to crawl into her lap.

"Lupe! Down," he scolded the dog fiercely.

"I don't mind." The woman laughed as the dog reached forward and licked at her chin and cheeks. She sputtered a bit when he licked across her mouth, leaning back and wiping her hand across her lips. "Slow down, big fella. We've just met."

"Lupe, come now." Jack patted his leg. The dog glanced at him, whined briefly and then turned back to the woman.

"Lupe!" Jack stared in disbelief at the dog. "Get over here now."

Blood heated his cheeks. He honestly wasn't sure if he was annoyed that the dog ignored him or jealous that Lupe had gotten to lick the woman's face.

With a final low whine, Lupe slunk back to Jack. He lay at his feet but kept his eyes trained on the woman's face.

"Sorry about that. I'm Jack." He held his hand out to the woman.

She stared at his outstretched hand. "I'm sorry, I don't shake hands. It's not you, it's -"

"Amelia." An older man with graying hair and a receding hairline crossed the office. Both Jack and Amelia stood as he stopped in front of them.

"Thank you for coming. I appreciate it." He glanced at Jack. "You must be Detective Emerson."

"I am. It's nice to meet you, Sheriff." Jack held out his hand.

The sheriff shook Jack's hand firmly. "I'm sorry to keep you waiting. I'm afraid I'll be just a little longer. We have a bit of a situation on our hands."

"I've heard. Anything I can help with?" Jack asked.

"Thanks, but no. We've got it covered." He held out his arm to Amelia, and she stepped in front of him. He followed her to the door that led to the main holding area.

"Have some coffee, Detective. I shouldn't be much longer," he called over his shoulder before he and Amelia disappeared behind the door.

* * *

"I'm sorry, Amelia. You know I wouldn't ask you if I wasn't desperate." Ray ran a hand through his thinning hair.

"I know, Ray." Amelia rubbed her hands together. Already, her stomach churned, but she ignored it as she followed the sheriff down the dingy corridor.

He stopped at the last door on the left. "Are you ready?"

She nodded and followed him into the bare, stark-looking room. The once white concrete walls had faded to dirty beige. The only furniture in the room was a brown wooden table and two chairs. Ed Morrison sat in one of the chairs. His arms were folded neatly on the table with his head resting on them. Amelia could smell the stench of liquor and tobacco radiating from his pores, even from across the room.

He looked up as Ray shut the door behind them and stared blearily at them. "Ms. Barlow? Why are you here?"

"Ray asked me to come. I want to talk to you about Julie and Wendy." Amelia sat in the chair opposite him and kept her hands clasped together in her lap.

His face drew together in a belligerent scowl. "I already told the sheriff I ain't got nothin' to do with that. I've been lookin' for them myself."

"Are you sure, Ed? You were pretty angry when Julie left you." Ray said.

"She's my wife. She promised to obey me, then took off with my kid. Of course, I was angry with her. But I didn't do nothin' to her." He exhaled loudly, and Amelia winced at his stale beer breath.

"It would be a hell of a lot easier on you if you told the truth for once in your sorry, miserable life, Ed," Ray said.

Ed's nostrils flared with anger. "You think you know everythin', don't ya, Sheriff? Think ya can bully me around, try to get me to confess to somethin' I didn't do just because yer the sheriff?"

He was becoming increasingly agitated, staring with something close to hatred at Ray standing at the end of the table. Quickly, before his attention switched back to her, Amelia grabbed Ed's wrists. Ed turned his gaze toward her as the confusion slowly turned to fear.

"Stop that," he whispered. "What are you doin' to me?"

Amelia didn't respond. She stared at him, and slowly, he leaned forward, staring blankly into her eyes. His hands twisted until he clasped Amelia's hands tightly in his own.

"Stop it," he whispered again before closing his eyes and dropping his head forward.

Amelia stared intently at the man across from her. Her body started to tremble, and a mixture of emotions flooded through her – revulsion, pity, fear and finally, anger. After a few minutes, she wrenched her hands free from Ed's grasp and placed them in her lap, where they twisted and pulled at her skirt.

Ed opened his eyes and stared at Amelia. His mouth opened and closed several times before he said in a low voice, "Richard?"

The colour drained from her cheeks, and her gorge rose. She swallowed hard and took a few deep breaths before turning to Ray. "He took them."

"Do you know where?" Ray asked.

"He has a cabin deep in the woods. Just after Miller's Crossing." She frowned. "We should take him with us. I think I could get us there, but it wasn't clear. If I need to, I can always ask him again."

Ray took Ed's arm. "C'mon, Ed. We're going to go for a little ride."

Ed shook himself like a dog after a rain shower and stared at the sheriff. "I don't know where they are. I swear to you."

"Don't bother, Ed. We know the truth now. You might as well help lead us in the right direction," Ray said.

"No, I ain't goin'. You can't make me tell you anything!" Ed shouted.

Amelia reached for him, and he jerked back, his face ashen.

"Don't you touch me," he moaned. "I can't stand it if you do."

"Tell you what, Ed." Ray leaned over until he was staring directly into Ed's bloodshot eyes. "You be a good boy and lead us to your wife and baby girl, and I won't ask Ms. Barlow here to touch you again."

Her stomach rolled and pitched like a boat in a storm.

Ray stared shrewdly at Ed. "Of course, if you don't want to cooperate, I just might need a bathroom break, and you'll be alone in this room with her."

"No!" Ed's body vibrated in the chair. "Don't leave me with her."

He stared at Amelia with his mouth turned down in disgust. "She's a witch. I know she is."

Amelia stood abruptly. "Excuse me, Sheriff."

She fled the room and hurried down the hallway. She pushed through the door into the office area. The walls were closing in on her, and she was close to fainting.

I just need fresh air. I just need fresh air. I just need fresh air.

She inwardly chanted that simple phrase like a prayer until she reached the front door and nearly fell onto the sidewalk. She put her hands on her knees and leaned over, dragging in breath after breath of the cool evening air.

Dimly, she was aware of the bell above the door chiming and then the hot breath of a dog on her face. Lupe whined and licked her face, and without stopping to think about it, she knelt and buried her face in his shaggy neck. Her hands tightened almost painfully onto the animal's shoulders, but if it hurt, he didn't attempt to move away. After a few moments, she calmed, and she raised her head, smiling as the dog licked her cheek again.

"Are you okay?"

Amelia shivered a little at the closeness of that deep voice. She looked to her left to see Jack kneeling beside her.

He's such a handsome man, she thought hazily.

His dark brown hair was thick and cut short. His tanned face boasted high cheekbones and a square jaw covered in a thick scruff of hair. And that voice. Every time he spoke, a little shiver moved down her spine. She stared in fascination at his warm golden brown eyes as they dropped to her mouth and darkened. His nostrils flared as he inhaled deeply. She licked her lips, and at the sight of her tongue, what sounded like a growl emerged from deep within his throat.

She realized with something like horror that he had leaned forward until his face was only inches from hers, and his large hand was almost cupping her face. With a loud and panicked squeak, she pushed backward, losing her balance and falling gracelessly onto her ass.

"Don't touch me!" she gasped as he reached to help her off the ground.

Eyes narrowing, he stood and stepped back as Amelia scrambled to her feet.

"I'm sorry. It's just - I don't like being touched. It's nothing personal." She bit her lip and stared down at Lupe, who sat at her feet and stared anxiously at her.

Jack shrugged. "No big deal."

She gave him a quick once-over. She was tall, nearly 5'10, but Jack still towered above her. She guessed he had to be at least 6'4, maybe bigger. He didn't seem to be bothered by her rejection. In fact, he looked almost bored with her now, and she tried to tell herself it wasn't disappointment she felt.

The bell chimed again, and Susan stepped out onto the sidewalk. "Amelia, are you okay?" She handed Amelia her gloves.

"I'm fine, thank you, Susan." She quickly tugged on her gloves, smoothing them over her arms as Jack held the door open, and she followed Susan back into the office.

Ray came out of the back area, followed by one of his deputies and a handcuffed and sullen Ed. "Amelia, can I get you anything?"

She shook her head. "No, I'm fine. I'm ready to go."

Ray glanced apologetically at Jack. "I'm sorry, Detective

Emerson, but I'm afraid I'll have to cancel our appointment until tomorrow."

"I was planning on heading back tonight. Do you mind if I tag along with you? We can meet after you've cleared up this other business," Jack said.

Ray, obviously anxious to get going, shrugged. "Sure, why not."

He stared at Ed and his deputy and then back at Jack. "Would you mind taking Amelia with you? We can get by with just one squad car if you do."

Jack nodded. "If Amelia is fine with it."

"Um…" Amelia fidgeted and bit at her bottom lip. She tried desperately to think of a reason why it wouldn't be a good idea, but unfortunately, *I can't go with him because I keep wondering how it would feel to have those big hands touching me,* wasn't something she could go blurting out to the entire Sheriff's department.

They were all staring at her now, Ray with a slight frown and Jack with those disconcerting brown eyes. She had a feeling he knew exactly what she was thinking, and she flushed a little. "That'll be fine. Thank you."

CHAPTER 2

"Take your next right." Amelia pointed at the dirt road, barely visible in the growing dusk.

As Jack turned right, she glanced behind her. Ray, his deputy Kevin, and Ed were in the squad car behind them, and she watched as Kevin signalled and followed Jack's truck down the bumpy road.

She giggled a little bit when Lupe licked the back of her head, and she placed one arm around the big dog, scratching the front of his chest. "You is such a good puppy. Yes, you is."

She nuzzled his neck with her face and then wiped the dog hair from her cheek. She was grateful, not just for the dog's calming presence, but because sitting in the middle of the truck, he made a welcome barrier between her and the large, silent man driving. She stared at Jack's hands. They were rough and callused looking and covered in tiny scars. As she wondered how exactly he had gotten those scars, she realized she was rubbing her scar and forced herself to stop.

"So, tell me, Amelia. What exactly is it that you do for the sheriff's department?" Jack asked.

"Well, I guess you could call me a consultant of sorts, Detective Emerson."

"Call me Jack." He peered at her over Lupe's large, shaggy head. "A consultant, huh? So… the sheriff needs a confession, and you come in and muscle it out of the suspect?"

She smiled a little. "I'm tougher than I look."

"I've no doubt of that. Still – you don't seem like the fighting type to me," he said.

She cleared her throat. "Let's just say that I have skills that allow me to discover people's secrets."

She stared out the window. The sun hadn't set yet, but they were deep in the woods, and it was already dark.

"Skills?" he mused. "I'd very much like to know what they are."

"They're really nothing that special. Forgive me, Jack, but I have to ask you to stop talking for a moment. I need to concentrate on where we are."

* * *

Jack inhaled deeply and tried to focus on his driving. It was nearly impossible. Amelia's scent filled the entire truck cab and drove him crazy. Her scent was affecting Lupe as well. The beast was affectionate with Jack and aloof with others. It had always been that way… until now. The animal was giving off his own unique scent, one that Jack recognized quickly. However, he had only previously smelled it when Lupe chased prey or was given a particularly tasty bone. It was the scent of pure, unrestrained joy.

Jack took another deep breath. Under that beautiful scent of vanilla and jasmine wafting from Amelia, there was another. A scent he'd discovered when he knelt beside her outside of the sheriff's office. She was practically swimming in arousal. She wanted him.

Even outside, with the cool wind blowing, the scent of her arousal had been strong and heady, and he'd reacted to it almost immediately. The closer he got to her, the stronger her arousal became, which is why he was so surprised when she pushed away from him and told him not to touch her. Despite her earlier rejection of him, the smell was still there, fainter now but detectable.

"Here – turn here." Amelia pointed to his left, and he slammed on the brakes. He peered out the window.

"Do you see a road?" she asked.

"Yeah, it's faint, just some dents in the weeds, but there's a trail."

He turned down it, the squad car following closely behind them. After about ten minutes of driving, they drove to a small wood cabin. Amelia vibrated on the seat with excitement, and as he put the truck in park and shut it off, she opened the door and jumped out of the cab.

"Amelia, wait!" Jack cursed under his breath and slid out of the truck. With Lupe at her heels, Amelia was already at the cabin door, pushing and pulling on the handle. It was locked with a large black padlock.

"Julie? Julie? Can you hear me?" she yelled through the door.

Ray and Kevin brought Ed to the cabin door. Ray searched through Ed's pockets until he pulled out a key. He handed it to Kevin, who quickly unlocked the padlock and pushed open the door. It was dark in the cabin, and he drew his gun before turning on the flashlight he pulled from his belt.

"She's in the bedroom. It's down the hall, second door on the right," Amelia said

The group hurried down the hallway. Jack had drawn his gun and nodded at Kevin, who quietly opened the door and swung it open. Jack entered the room and looked around.

"The woman's on the bed."

Ray grunted. "How the hell do you know that? We can't see a damn thing in here."

Jack didn't reply as Kevin shone the flashlight on the bed, illuminating a woman huddled under the covers.

"Julie!" Before Jack could stop her, Amelia ran to the woman and threw back the covers. She was pale and still but made a soft moaning sound when the chilly air washed over her.

"She's still alive." Amelia sat on the bed beside the petite blonde woman. "Julie, honey, can you hear me?"

Ray shoved Ed to the floor with an angry snarl. "What did you do to her?"

"Nothin'!" Ed squealed. "I swear to you she was fine when I left. I didn't even hit her. I just locked her and Wendy in the cabin, and then I left."

Amelia searched the bed for the baby. "Wendy's not here, Ed."

"She has to be," Ed whined. "She was in her mama's arms when I left."

Jack sniffed the air delicately. Beside him, Lupe did the same – the two of them repeatedly inhaling as Amelia glanced at him.

"Jack?" she said.

"Something isn't right." Jack bent over the bed and rolled the woman onto her back. The woman was ashen, and her body ice cold.

"Sheriff - your flashlight," Jack said.

Ray tossed Jack his flashlight, and he aimed the light on the woman's face and neck. Amelia squinted at Julie's throat. "Is that? What are those? Needle marks?"

She pointed to the two small pinholes on Julie's throat. There was a ring of dried blood around each of them.

Shit.

Jack straightened and took Amelia by one glove-covered arm. He hauled her to her feet as Lupe growled low in his throat.

Jack glanced at the others. "We have to leave - now."

"No, wait!" Amelia wrenched her arm free. "We need to help Julie and find Wendy."

"It's too late. She's dying," Jack said quietly as Ray approached the bed.

"She's still alive," Amelia said.

"Not for long. We need to go now," Jack said. "She's barely breathing, Amelia."

Amelia shook free of his grip and stripped off her gloves. She laid her hands on the woman's cold, pale face. She closed her eyes but yanked her hands off the woman within seconds.

She looked up at Ray, her face already streaked with tears. "Wendy – she's in the closet." She pointed to the door across the room.

Ray crossed the room and opened the door. A tiny baby lay on the floor in a nest of blankets. She slept peacefully with one small fist curled up against her cheek. Ray picked her up and carried her to the others. "She's alive. Seems okay to me."

Julie made one final gasp, her eyes staring sightlessly at the ceiling. Ed moaned from his spot on the floor. "Julie? Baby?"

"Shit," Ray groaned. "We need to get the coroner out here."

Lupe began to growl. His hackles raised, and he bared his teeth as he stared at the window.

"We need to leave right now, Sheriff. We can come back for the woman in the morning," Jack said.

"Are you crazy?" Ray said. "I don't know how you work in

17

the city, but here, there are procedures to follow. We can't just -"

"Jack's right," Amelia said. She backed away from the bed and stood in front of the window to the right of the bed. "Ray, what happened to Julie - it wasn't Ed. I can't. I mean, I don't even know how to begin to explain it, but we should leave right now."

She screamed when the window exploded behind her. Long pale arms circled her waist. Before the others could react, she was yanked through the window and vanished into the darkness. Jack roared in shock and surprise as Lupe, snarling and barking, leaped through the broken window after her.

He turned to the sheriff. "Get to the car now!" He shoved the sheriff in the direction of the door. "Hurry! Get in the car and get the hell out of here!"

"Amelia - we can't leave her," Ray said as Kevin hauled Ed to his feet and pushed him out the door.

"I'll find her. Go!" Jack shouted.

Ray turned and stumbled for the door, clutching the infant to his chest.

Jack jumped out the broken window, tearing off his jacket as he landed on the ground. He dropped his gun beside the jacket and inhaled deeply. He ran toward Amelia's scent, stripping off his shirt as he ran deep into the forest.

CHAPTER 3

"What do we have here?" The man said as he pushed Amelia back against the tree. Moving in a blur of speed, the man had carried her deep into the forest, holding her like she was weightless.

His hand pressed against her stomach, and she could feel the coldness from his flesh seeping through the thin material of her tank top. She kept her hands well away from him. There wasn't a chance in hell she was touching this man - this *thing* - in front of her.

"You're a pretty little thing, aren't you, Amelia?" He went to stroke her cheek, and she yanked her head back.

"How do you know my name?" she asked, her voice shaking.

"I've been blessed with an excellent sense of hearing. I was preparing to leave my new friend when I heard you and your friends arriving. I decided I would stick around for some dessert. And I am so thrilled I did."

He leaned forward and inhaled deeply. "You smell delicious, my pet."

He frowned and sniffed again. "I've never smelled anything like you before. What are you?"

Amelia could barely breathe. Adrenaline shot through her veins, making her limbs shake and her heart thump painfully in her chest. The man standing in front of her, holding her immobile with only one long-fingered hand, was so pale his skin was nearly translucent. He had jet-black hair swept back from his forehead in an old-fashioned style, and his face was thin with sharp cheekbones and a proud aristocratic nose.

He shrugged at her silence, his thin shoulders moving delicately in his black suit jacket. "It doesn't matter. You smell delicious - you'll taste delicious."

He grinned at her, and Amelia screamed at the sight of the long fangs protruding from his mouth. Chuckling, the creature bent his head and latched onto her neck, sinking his fangs deep into the throbbing vein in her throat. Amelia screamed again. She could hear the creature grunting with pleasure as he suckled at her neck.

She moaned as the vampire's thoughts and feelings filled her mind in bright flashes of terrible blue light. She wanted to die. Never had she felt such horrifying thoughts and desires before. Just when she believed she would go insane, the creature released her neck with a loud, wet, popping sound.

"What was that?" The vampire panted harshly, his mouth ringed with her blood. He licked delicately at his lips. "Such power you have. What a marvellous gift you've been given. Tell me – how ever did you acquire it?"

When she refused to answer, he grinned a little. "All right then, perhaps you'll share who Richard is?"

She flinched but stayed silent, and he laughed. "I can't decide if I should drain you now or keep you as my pet. Let's have another drink while I decide, shall we?"

He leaned forward, but before he could sink his teeth into

her, a loud snarling filled the air, and he was knocked away from her. She stumbled and collapsed against the tree, dropping to her knees as the vampire staggered and fell. Lupe stood in front of her, growling viciously. He bared his teeth, and any resemblance to the friendly dog licking her face in the sheriff's office was completely gone.

The vampire leaped gracefully to his feet. He brushed bits of dead leaves and pine needles from his suit pants before grinning delightedly. "My pet has a pet! A human with a wolf as a guardian - this gets better and better. I have a feeling I'm going to like it here."

He moved slowly towards Lupe, almost seeming to float in the air. "You'd better call your dog off, my pretty one. Unless you want to watch it die a truly agonizing death."

Lupe's growling grew louder, and he crouched. He was preparing to leap at the pale creature before him, and Amelia moaned in dismay. "Lupe, no."

The dog wouldn't stand a chance against the creature. She had witnessed his power and speed and felt the horrible things he could do. Only death waited for Lupe.

Before Lupe could launch himself at the creature, there was a low rustling in the bushes to Amelia's left. She cringed back against the tree as a massive wolf, he made Lupe look like a puppy, emerged from the darkness. His green eyes glowed in the dark, and a low growl rumbled deep within his chest.

The vampire bared his fangs and hissed at the beast. "I don't fear you, Lycan. Your kind grows weaker every day while mine only grows stronger."

Despite his words, he stepped back as the wolf, and Lupe moved toward him.

His eyes flickered to Amelia. "What is she? A Lycan and a wolf both protecting her? She must be special."

He licked his lips as he slowly stepped backward. "I've

tasted her, dog. I know of her powers. They make her," he paused and inhaled deeply, "particularly tasty."

Amelia clapped her hands over her ears when the giant wolf howled deafeningly. Before the big wolf's howl had ended, a chorus of howls answered his call from within the forest's depths. A flicker of fear showed in the vampire's eyes for the first time.

"I'll be seeing you again, my pet." He blew a kiss to Amelia and then turned and fled into the forest. The wolf snarled and chased after him, disappearing into the dark. Amelia huddled on the ground for a moment. Her heart raced like a runaway train in her chest, and she could hear a weird buzzing in her ears. She shrieked in fear and surprise when a cold, wet nose nudged her arm. She looked up to see Lupe sitting in front of her and panting. She wrapped her arms around the dog's chest and breathed deeply.

"We have to go, Lupe. Come on. Take me to Jack," she murmured. Using the dog to steady herself, she stood up. She felt light-headed almost immediately and plopped back onto her butt.

"Shit," she muttered and stuck her head between her knees. She tried to think. The blood the vampire had taken from her had left her weak and disoriented. She would never make it back to the cabin.

"Lupe, can you find Jack? Be a good boy, and go find Jack." She said.

She lifted her head and stared pleadingly at the dog. "Go on, boy. Go find Jack for me."

The dog only stared at her with his head cocked to the side.

Groaning, she rose to her feet and, clutching the tree behind her for support, attempted to take a few shaky steps. The earth tilted alarmingly under her feet, but as she crumpled to the ground, she was caught and cradled against a hard chest.

"It's okay, Amelia. I have you." Jack's quiet rumble was music to her ears.

She squinted at Jack. He wavered in and out of focus, and darkness crept in on her vision.

"Don't touch -" she managed before the darkness claimed her.

CHAPTER 4

A melia sighed. The heart beneath her ear beat a steady rhythm, and her body seemed to sway in gentle response to it. She sighed again and snuggled closer, one hand creeping up to wrap around a powerful neck. She could feel coarse chest hair against her cheek, and she rubbed the side of her face against it delicately. She shivered as a cool wind bit into her bare back where her tank top had ridden up, and she was shifted and held more firmly.

So nice, she thought dreamily. The motion reminded her of being a child and her father scooping her up and carrying her to her bed. It had been so long since she'd felt the warmth and touch of another human. The last time was ten years ago when Richard –

Amelia's eyes flew open. She was cradled against a warm, hard chest and carried through the darkness. She struggled, and Jack's voice washed over her. "It's okay, Amelia. You're safe. You're fine."

"Jack?" She craned her neck over his shoulder and saw Lupe following behind them. "Lupe found you. Good puppy."

Jack shifted her higher, and she tucked her head against

his throat for a moment. She still felt tired and weak, and the heat radiating from Jack's body made her sleepy. She traced one finger over his bare shoulder, feeling the muscles below the smoothness of his skin.

"Why are you so hot?" she asked. "Your skin is -"

She stopped as the realization of what was happening sunk in. She twisted and squirmed against him so violently he nearly dropped her. "Put me down! Right now! Jack, put me down!"

Cursing, he dropped her to her feet, but as soon as he let go of her, a wave of dizziness washed over her. She lurched forward, and Jack grabbed her by her forearms.

"No," she begged, "don't...."

She paused, staring at Jack's hands on her arms.

"Amelia? Do you feel faint?" Jack asked.

She shook her head. "Jack, do you feel me?"

"Of course, I feel you." He rubbed her upper arms. "You feel freezing."

She reached up and placed her trembling hands on his cheeks.

"Amelia, what are you doing?" he asked.

"Shh, just be quiet for a minute," she said.

He did as she asked. She stood quietly for more than a minute, staring intensely at him. Holy crap... she couldn't feel him.

"Amelia?" Jack said.

"I can't feel you," she said.

"What do you mean?" He touched her hands. "Are your hands that numb?"

"I can't feel you," she repeated. She traced one hand down his throat and pressed it against his chest directly over his heart. She felt his heartbeat increase at the gentle pressure of her skin against his.

A child-like grin of delight crossed her face. "You're blank to me. I can't feel anything."

"Amelia, I have no idea what you mean, but we need to go. You've lost a lot of blood, and it's getting colder. We need to get you to the hospital."

She pulled back a little, the look of delight still on her face, and looked down at his body. "What is it that makes you different? Why can't I feel…."

A hot blush flooded through her, and she almost forgot for a moment that she couldn't feel Jack's emotions or thoughts. She stared at his body for another ten seconds before gazing at his face. "Jack? Why are you naked?"

* * *

THE VAMPIRE FLED THROUGH THE FOREST. THE BLOOD FROM the woman hummed and buzzed through his veins. He had the same high he always had after feeding, but this one felt more profound and intense, and he trembled excitedly. The woman, this Amelia, was a rarity he had never tasted before, and he would do whatever it took to taste her again. He wondered if –

He skidded to an abrupt halt. He could see in the darkness better than a cat, and it took only a moment for him to realize that he was surrounded.

He felt a touch of fear, but he pasted a cocky smile onto his face and gave a short bow. "Gentlemen, I am the vampire, Julian."

He forced himself to stand steady as the seven large Lycans grew closer and surrounded him in a tight circle. He held up his hands. "My friends, I mean you no harm."

The Lycan in front of him snarled, revealing large, razor-sharp teeth.

Julian took a step backwards. "I have no quarrel with you. I am merely travelling through. I swear."

He watched as the Lycan transformed into his human form. A tall and muscular man with a long, ropy scar across his chest stared at him. "These woods belong to us, bloodsucker."

"But of course. I did not mean to trespass." He backed away from the man, but a low growl behind him made him whirl to face the other Lycans.

"Gentlemen, please." His nose wrinkled in disgust at the Lycans' smell. "I am new to the area. Surely you will provide leniency to a tired traveller?"

He stiffened in alarm as the man's hands wrapped around his neck. "We show no mercy for your kind. The penalty for invading our forest is death. You should -"

The man stopped. Julian shook in his grip as images from the Lycan invaded his head. He moaned quietly as the Lycan released him and shoved him to the ground. Breathing hard, the Lycan stared at his hands and the vampire at his feet.

"What sorcery is this?" he said.

The other Lycans quickly shifted, and the smallest one, a redhead covered in freckles, approached him. "Anthony, what is it?"

"I'm not sure, Eric." He stared at Julian. "How did you do that?"

Julia kept his mouth shut.

"What did he do?" Eric stared at Julian before reaching toward him.

"No!" Anthony shouted. "Don't touch him. We take him back to David."

He leaned over Julian, snarling low in his throat. "On your feet, bloodsucker. I am showing you mercy in not tearing your head off right here – do not make me regret it."

Moving as one, the Lycans herded Julian deeper into the

forest. After twenty minutes of walking, they arrived at a large clearing in the woods. One large cabin and three smaller ones were scattered throughout the clearing, with six additional cabins nestled among the trees just outside of it.

The door to the largest cabin swung open, and a man stepped out, ducking his head to clear the doorway. Julian stared at him. He was huge – standing over seven feet tall with a broad chest and powerful arms and legs. His skin was a light brown and covered in a fine coating of hair as if, even in human form, the wolf in him could not be contained.

The Lycans surrounding him bowed deeply before Anthony approached him. "David, I must speak with you. This creature has -"

With a roar, David swung one meaty arm and caught the unsuspecting Anthony across the jaw. The Lycan flew across the clearing before smashing into a large pine tree.

"You bring this vermin into our home?" David snarled. He strode across the clearing and wrapped his hand around the fallen Lycan's neck. He lifted him easily until Anthony was face-to-face with him, his feet dangling and his face an alarming purple shade.

"You bring this bloodsucker to our doorstep - where our mates and pups are?" he roared.

"Please, David," Anthony choked out. "This one is different. He has strange powers – interesting powers. I thought you would want to know."

Julian watched as David's hand squeezed mercilessly around the Lycan's throat. The Lycan was turning blue, and his struggles were weakening. With one final squeeze, David tossed him to the ground like a rag doll. He leaned over the wheezing, choking man.

"You had better hope the vermin's power is as interesting as you claim them to be."

Anthony raised one hand to his throat and rubbed at the redness. "Touch him," he said hoarsely.

With a low growl, David turned and stalked back to Julian. Julian flinched when David reached out and gripped the vampire's arm. After a moment, he turned back to Anthony. "You dare lie to me?"

"Skin – touch his skin," Anthony rasped.

The Lycan wrapped one ham-like hand around Julian's thin neck, sighing heavily through his nose. Immediately, images from David flooded Julian's brain. He stared wide-eyed at the Lycan as David's nostrils flared and his tanned skin grew pale. With a loud snort, he let go of Julian's neck.

"Your kind disgusts me," he said. "The way you need the humans to survive. Your very existence relies on their blood."

He rubbed his hands disgustedly against his pants as if he could wipe away the images he had received from Julian. "Tell me, little ant, where did you get this power?"

When Julian stayed silent, David grabbed and shook him by his coat. "I asked you a question. Answer it."

"A woman, a human named Amelia. I fed on her," Julian whimpered. His brain still reeled with the images of his enemy's life. Disturbing images of the vampires David had killed were burned into Julian's brain. With sudden, brutal clarity, he realized that the woman's powers were not a gift but a terrible curse.

He moaned when the Lycan began to shift. His brown eyes glowed with terrible yellow light, and his body expanded with every breath he took. His shirt ripped along his arms with a soft purring sound, and Julian cried out when David's fingers lengthened, and the fingernails turned to claws.

"Is this Amelia, the woman you fed on tonight?" The Lycan grinned at him.

Julian nodded frantically. A beard sprouted on the Lycan's

face, and his white teeth grew larger by the second. "I fed on her. I – I must have absorbed some of her powers."

He was babbling now – the words tumbling from his throat.

"Who were those men you saw with her?" The Lycan frowned as hair sprouted from his forehead. "Already the images from you are fading… answer me." He squeezed Julian's arms, ignoring his squeal of pain.

"The one in the uniform was the sheriff," he moaned. "Another was one of your kind."

David released Julian, and he fell to the ground. He stayed on his knees as the Lycan turned to Anthony. "We find this woman… this Amelia. I wish to know more about this power."

"Couldn't we just keep the bloodsucker?" Anthony asked, his voice still hoarse.

Fresh, hot fear exploded in Julian at the thought of being kept as the Lycan's pet.

"Once the woman's blood is no longer in his system, the power will fade. He will be useless to us," David said.

Julian nodded eagerly. "It is true. Already, the abilities are not as powerful as they were."

He peered up at the Lycan standing before him. "I ask for mercy from you. Let me go, and I will leave your lands forever. I promise."

David laughed derisively. "If it is mercy you ask for, then it is mercy you'll receive. A quick and painless death for you, I think."

His last few words became a snarl, and Julian screamed in terror as the man finished his transformation into beast. He howled triumphantly into the night sky and tore Julian's head from his neck with one sweep of his paw. He howled again, and the others around him answered his call as Julian's headless body turned to ash.

CHAPTER 5

"Jack? Why are you naked?" Amelia repeated. She looked up at him, her face flaming with colour.

"I'll explain later. C'mon, we need to go." Without waiting for her response, he scooped her up in his arms again, ignoring her small squeak, and headed toward the cabin. He walked quickly, and Lupe loped along at his side.

Amelia could feel her face growing hotter. She was being carried through the forest by a huge, very *naked* man, and every one of her nerve endings sang in response. The worst part was that she couldn't seem to stop touching him. Although her mind was nearly screaming at her to stop, after a decade of avoiding everyone's touch, her hands politely ignored her brain and ran their fingers over the smooth skin of his back and shoulders.

As Jack strode through the forest, she again marvelled at his warmth. A chilly wind blew, and the smaller trees in the woods bent and swayed, but the heat from Jack's body warmed her from her head to her toes. Still blushing, knowing she should stop but unable to, she continued to run the tips of her fingers over his upper back.

She traced his collarbone with her right hand and then into the heavy mat of hair on his chest. The hair was coarse, and she rubbed a bit of it experimentally between her fingers before sliding her hand to the small scar on the left side of his chest. She traced it gently, then placed her palm flat over the skin. She could feel his heart beating solidly. When her left hand, which seemed to have a mind of its own, ran up the back of his neck and threaded through the thick hair on his skull, she actually felt the beat increase.

She sneaked a glance at his face. He stared straight ahead into the darkness. Although nothing was on his face to suggest that he was even aware of her roaming hands, she could see the pulse thudding heavily in his throat.

Amelia swallowed. There was a new sensation in her belly. A dull, aching throb that spread from her abdomen down until it settled in the area between her thighs. Her skin was suddenly deliciously sensitive, and the bottom half of her body felt heavy and full. She twitched her legs a little, trying to relieve some of the strange pressure she felt, and Jack shifted her higher. His hand tightened around the back of her thighs, and she gasped quietly. His other hand gripped her around the ribcage just below her breast, and she had the strangest urge to grab that hand and move it up until it was touching her breast. The thought of his hand on her breast made her nipples harden, and she stared again at the pulse in his throat.

Her right hand slipped across his chest and over one of his nipples while her left hand curled into his hair and gripped tightly. She circled the flat nipple with her thumb. It hardened under her touch, and she shivered. Desire coursed through her body, making her breasts swell and her core ache with new intensity.

If you put your hand down there, you would be soaking wet.

Unbidden, a vision of Jack's hard, warm hand between

34

her thighs rose in her mind, and a spasm of sudden, intense pleasure in her belly made her shudder violently against him.

"Are you okay?" Jack rumbled in his deep voice.

"Fine," she whispered. She couldn't stop staring at the pulse on his neck. A small drop of moisture was sliding down his neck toward his collarbone, and she watched it with fascination. Her lips parted, and she leaned forward, placing her mouth against his throat. She licked away the drop and felt, more than heard, his sharp intake of breath.

"Jesus. Amelia, stop." His voice, full of an emotion she couldn't identify, broke through her haze of lust. She leaned back, suddenly and utterly horrified at her behaviour.

"Oh my God! Jack, I'm sorry. I don't know why I – I did that," she said as he eased her to the ground.

She stared at the ground, wondering if she would be lucky enough to have it simply open and swallow her whole, but it stayed stubbornly closed beneath her feet. Lupe sat down beside her, pushing his large head into her hand.

"Just give me a minute," Jack grunted.

He turned away from her, and although she willed herself to keep her eyes firmly on Lupe's head, they glanced upward anyway. She bit her lip hard. Her face was so hot she was sure it was glowing in the darkness. Before Jack turned away, she caught sight of his large, very erect penis, and now a slew of emotions churned in her stomach.

Embarrassment topped the list, followed closely by curiosity, but there was also another unfamiliar wave of aching fullness through her lower body that made her skin tingle and her breathing quicken.

Blood loss. It's obviously from the blood loss, shock, and realization that there's someone out there I can touch. It's not surprising I would find him so fascinating.

Jack picked up his jeans from the forest floor, shook them

out, and slipped into them. He kept his back turned to her as he zipped and buttoned them.

He turned around and stared at her. "Can you walk? It's not much farther to the cabin, but I can carry you if you can't."

"No, I can walk."

He held his hand out, and after a brief moment of hesitation, she took his hand. Without looking at her, he started walking again. Feeling a little lightheaded, she hurried after him.

* * *

JACK WALKED QUICKLY, GRIMACING AS HIS DICK SCRAPED across the front of his jeans with every step he took. He was still as hard as a rock and silently thanked God that Amelia had chosen to walk. She was slowing them down a bit. He could move faster and quieter if he picked her up again, but at this point, it was a chance they'd have to take. The smell of her need and desire for him surrounded them like a thick blanket. He didn't entirely trust that he could stop himself from taking her right there on the ground if he had to carry her again.

He took shallow breaths and tried to ignore the woman beside him, but he kept reliving the touch of her hands on his body, the feel of her mouth and her small pink tongue tasting his skin. Maybe he could convince her to have a quickie once they returned to his truck. Just enough to take the edge off and lessen the need for them both.

Jesus, he needed to get control of himself. A dead woman was in the cabin just ahead of them, and a vampire was on the loose. Not to mention some of his kind and quite a few, judging by their answering howls. The woman he was thinking about having sex with in the front seat of his truck had been bitten and was weak from blood loss. Plus, there was the fact that his kind, generally speaking, didn't mate with humans. It wasn't strictly forbidden, but there was an unspoken agreement that human women would weaken the bloodlines and, therefore, were considered less desirable than Lycan women. Of course, he mused, he didn't have much choice. A Lycan female would never mate with a half-breed.

The wind gusted, and he wrinkled his nose. The blood-sucker's scent was still on Amelia, nearly buried beneath her scent and the smell of her need, but he would convince her to give him an article of her clothing. He could use it to track down the bloodsucker. He was positive it was the one he had come to this small town looking for. The sooner he disposed of the murderous cockroach, the better.

He stopped, and Amelia ran into his back.

"I'm so sorry," she squeaked again and dropped his hand before retreating a safe distance. He bent and pulled on his left boot, searching in the darkness for the right. It was nearly hidden under a bush, and he pulled it free of the branches with a grunt of effort and pushed his foot into it.

"Let's go," he said impatiently and held out his hand again. She took it, and he led her about another ten feet before stopping again. This time, it was his shirt, flung carelessly onto a low branch of a tree, and he yanked it down and shoved his arms into it, buttoning it quickly before they moved forward again.

He could see the cabin ahead of them, and Amelia must have seen the dark outline even with her human sight because she sighed in relief and moved a little faster.

He could smell her exhaustion. She was undoubtedly freezing now that she didn't have his body heat. She was shaking wildly, but Jack shook his head and pulled her to a stop when she started toward the front of the cabin. "Careful, there's broken glass everywhere."

She stayed where she was, her shaking increasing as he crunched his way over the glass and picked up his jacket and gun. He closed the outside shutters on the broken window and latched it shut before walking back to her. He dropped his coat over her shoulders, and she slipped her arms into it with a slight nod of thanks. It was comically oversized on her. The sleeves fell past her hands, and the jacket hem hung to her knees, but she zipped it up to her chin. He took her hand and led her around the side of the small cabin, moving confidently in the darkness.

"What about Ray and Kevin?" she asked when he tugged her toward his truck.

"They should be back at the sheriff's department by now. I told them to take Ed and the baby and leave," he said.

"We can't leave Julie here," she said.

He glanced back at her. "There isn't anything we can do for her now. We'll send the coroner out in the morning. It's not safe here, Amelia. We have to go."

They were at the truck now, and he opened the door and lifted her into it. She scooted over to the middle as Lupe leaped in after her, and Jack shut the door. He slid behind the wheel and started the truck. He turned the heat on high, angling the vents, so they pointed directly at her and then drove away from the cabin.

CHAPTER 6

They drove for maybe five minutes when Amelia said quietly, "That thing was a vampire."

When he didn't reply, she rushed on. "I know it sounds insane, but he had fangs, and he bit me, Jack. He bit me."

She lifted her chin and showed him the marks on her neck. "He was going to bite me again, and then Lupe showed up and knocked him away."

She put her arm around the dog and scratched between his shoulder blades. He licked her face, whining softly, and she rested her forehead against him. "I knew you were a good puppy. Yes, I did."

She glanced back at Jack. "And then something else showed up. The vampire called it a Lycan. It was like a big wolf. I mean, really big and scary, and it chased the vampire into the woods."

When he stayed quiet, she said, "I'm not crazy."

"I know you're not crazy, and yes, it was a vampire," he said.

His simple acknowledgement stunned her into silence for a moment. "You believe me?"

"Yes. That thing was what brought me to your town in the first place. I've been tracking it from a string of deaths in my city."

"Am I going to turn into a vampire now?" Fear made her voice thin.

"No. The only way you would turn is if he forced you to drink his blood. If he only bit you, then you're just suffering from blood loss. I'm taking you to the hospital. A blood transfusion will help you feel better."

"No," she said sharply. "I can't go to the hospital."

He frowned at her. "You can, and you will. Amelia, you need a blood transfusion. You're probably suffering from mild hypothermia, and those bite marks will need to be cleaned."

The panic clawed at her throat, her breathing quickening until she was nearly hyperventilating. Years of deliberately avoiding people had given her more than a touch of agora-phobia, and the thought of being in a hospital, where people were paid to touch you and examine you, made her skin crawl.

"Jack, let me out of the truck." She tried to squirm past Lupe.

"What? No. You're not getting out of the truck. We're in the middle of nowhere." He took her arm and held her in place next to him.

The panic eating at her common sense, she punched at his ribs. He muttered a curse as the truck swerved on the road. "What the hell, Amelia?"

"Let go of me, Jack! I mean it! I am not going to the hospi-tal. Stop the truck and let me out. I'll walk from here!"

Her breath whistled in and out of the pinhole her throat had turned into. He growled when one of her flailing hands caught him in the jaw.

He stepped on the brakes and threw the truck into park.

She stopped flailing at him and lunged around Lupe for the door. Jack put his arms around her waist and pulled her back until she sat on his lap, wedged between his body and the steering wheel.

"Let go of me, you asshole!" she shouted and tried to punch him in the face.

He wrapped his arms around her, pinning her arms to her body. She wriggled and squirmed as he made weirdly soothing soft growls and refused to release her. Exhausted and beginning to cry, she collapsed against him.

He loosened his grip around her, but all the fight had left her. She rested her head on his chest and slipped her arms around his neck, clinging to him weakly as tears dripped down her face.

"Please don't take me to the hospital, Jack. I'm fine. I promise you. I can't – I can't have all those people touching me," she said.

He rubbed her back through the thick material of his jacket. "I won't take you to the hospital."

Amelia sniffed and wiped her face with her hand. "Thank you."

She leaned against Jack, breathing in his good, clean scent while he rubbed her back. She had forgotten how good a hug could feel - the simple pleasure of someone putting their arms around you. How nice it was to lean against someone and feel nothing but the beat of their heart under your cheek. She smoothed down the small hairs on the back of Jack's neck, making his hands momentarily squeeze her back. She realized she was finally warm. The heat in the truck and Jack's body heat had banished the chill from her bones.

She leaned back and looked up at him. "I'm sorry. I don't normally cry."

He studied her before one big hand cupped her face. He used his thumb to wipe the moisture from her cheek. She

41

caught her breath when his hand brushed against her mouth. His face was very close to hers now, and she licked her suddenly dry lips, making him groan and cup the back of her neck under her hair.

* * *

JACK STARED AT AMELIA. HER INTENSE AROUSAL FILLED THE truck, and his dick responded eagerly. It hardened against his zipper, and he studied her mouth intently. When her lips parted, he growled and pulled her face toward his, mashing his mouth down on hers and kissing her hungrily. She gasped, and he thrust his tongue into her mouth. She tasted like the sweetest honey, and he made a low growl of happiness. When she tried to pull back, he tightened his grip on her neck and angled his mouth over hers so he could explore all of her warm mouth with his tongue.

She dug her nails into his chest as he kissed her repeatedly, her mouth opening to his insistent tongue. She was still sitting sideways on his lap, and he lifted her easily and rearranged her so that she straddled him. He grabbed her hips and pushed her down against him, grinding his pelvis against her so that she could feel how hard he was for her. She cried out and clutched at the hard muscles in his shoulders as he kissed the line of her jaw and then sucked hard on her earlobe.

"Jack, I think …."

He yanked down the zipper on his jacket and cupped one full breast in his hand, pinching her nipple through the fabric of her tank top and bra. She gasped, her back arching into his touch.

He claimed her mouth again and, after a moment, said, "Kiss me, Amelia."

She hesitated and then kissed him in a shy and awkward

kind of way. He was puzzled by her timidity. She obviously wanted him and would have to be blind not to see how much he wanted her. He slid his hand under her tank top and worked his fingers under the cup of her bra. He wanted to feel her bare skin, wanted to feel her nipple hardening against the palm of his hand, but she stopped the chaste kisses she was giving him and grabbed at his arm.

"Jack, wait. I -"

Lights from an oncoming vehicle splashed over the truck, bathing them in light, and he could see how red her face was and how shy and uncomfortable she looked. Confused and slightly ashamed of himself, he lifted her off his lap and sat her on the seat beside him.

The car screeched to a stop beside them, and Ray jumped out as Jack lowered his window. His face was pale and worried, and he reached past Jack, trying to grab Amelia's hand.

"Amelia? Are you okay? Are you hurt?" he asked anxiously.

She pulled back from him. "I'm fine, Ray. I'm sorry. I'm not wearing my gloves." She avoided his reaching fingers.

He stopped. "Of course. I'm sorry, I forgot. I was so worried." He stared at Jack. "Did you catch the guy?"

"No. He got away. Where are Ed and the baby?"

"They're back at the office. I dropped Kevin off with them and then turned around and started back. I didn't know if I should bring backup or get out here as quickly as possible. This is one hell of a clusterfuck. We need to get the coroner out to the cabin," he said.

"Not tonight. Julie's not going anywhere, and I need to get Amelia home," Jack said.

"She has to make a statement. Bring her back to the office," Ray said.

"She can do it in the morning," Jack said.

Ray rubbed tiredly at his face. "Yeah, all right. This whole thing has turned into a giant shit show, anyway. Amelia, I'll drive you back to your place, and then, Jack, if you're still up to it, we can talk."

"I'll make sure she gets home safely," Jack said. "It's been a long day for everyone. If you have time, I'll chat with you tomorrow."

Ray frowned. "I thought you were leaving tonight."

"I'm going to stick around for a while longer. I'll talk to you in the morning about my reasons."

"Sure. Amelia, I'll send Kevin for you in the morning," Ray said.

"I'll pick her up and bring her to the office," Jack said.

Ray studied Amelia. "Is that all right with you, Amelia?"

"Yes," Amelia said.

"You sure?" Ray said.

Jack tried not to take it personally. Ray didn't know him from a fucking hole in the ground.

"Positive," Amelia said with a glance at Jack.

"All right. Drive safe. I'll see you tomorrow." Ray climbed into his car and drove off slowly as Jack shifted the truck into gear and followed him.

They drove in silence for a few minutes. Jack pretended not to notice Amelia sliding over until she was pressed against Lupe, putting as much space between them as possible.

"What are you, Amelia?" he asked.

"Wha – what do you mean?" she said.

"You wear these weird arm-length evening gloves. You won't shake hands with me when we first meet. The sheriff calls you in to talk to a criminal, and you somehow get information from said criminal. You touch a nearly dead woman and know immediately that her baby is in the closet. Oh, and then when I do touch you, you start babbling about how you can't feel me and spend the next fifteen minutes with your hands all over me."

He looked over at her. "Does that about cover it?"

She refused to look at him. Her hands were buried deep in Lupe's fur, and her face was hidden against his shoulder.

"So, I'm going to ask you again – what are you, Amelia?"

"I'm a freak, okay?" she snapped.

"Explain what you are, and I'll decide if I believe you're a freak," he said.

She blew her breath out angrily. "I don't *know* what I am. When I was sixteen, I was in a car accident with my twin brother, Richard. He died instantly," she paused, struggling to hold back the tears, "and I was hit in the head with a piece of the truck that we hit. I broke my leg and was in a coma for two weeks, and when I woke up, I was a freak. My mother hugged me, and her thoughts and feelings flooded through me. She was happy I was alive, I could feel that, but underneath that emotion, a single thread of thought was running on a loop in her brain. I screamed, I couldn't help it, and I haven't touched either of my parents since."

"What was the thought?" Jack asked quietly.

She swallowed, and his glance at her was more than enough to see the pain and suffering on her face. "She wished it had been Richard who lived."

"Christ, I'm sorry."

She wiped the tears from her face. "I thought, *hoped*, that maybe it was just because I had been in a coma, you know? That once I healed fully, I wouldn't be able to feel people's thoughts anymore. The month I spent in the hospital was agony. Having people touching me every day was horrible. I knew their deepest thoughts and their most shameful secrets. My night nurse was having an affair with one of the doctors. She was a nice lady, but her thoughts were...." Amelia trailed off and shuddered wildly.

45

After a moment, she said, "The secret was tearing her apart. And every time she touched me, I was privy to her desire for the doctor. I knew everything they did in bed together, the way she secretly liked the nasty names he called her when they had sex, how she let him tie her down and – and hurt her."

She paused with her mouth drawn down in a little moue of disgust. "She was addicted to the doctor and what he did to her, but underneath it all – the shame she felt was horrible. It coated her entire thoughts. I left the hospital and prayed that it would get better, but it got worse. Ray came to the house to interview me about the accident, and he touched my hand before I could stop him. That's when I discovered that now, not only could I feel other people's emotions and thoughts, they could feel mine."

"Jesus," Jack said.

"It's not the same for everyone. Smart people, like Ray, can feel all of my emotions and hear my thoughts. Less intelligent people generally get an idea of my emotions, or maybe they just get a weird feeling when they touch me. I don't know exactly what it is, only that it scares them, makes them look at me like I'm a freak."

He frowned. "Are you telling me that Ray figured out your abilities and uses them to his advantage? Uses them to help him do his job?"

She shook her head. "No, it's not like that."

His hands clenched around the steering wheel. "I'll talk with Ray tomorrow morning. He shouldn't be using you to help his career."

"Stop it." She glared at him. "Ray isn't like that. He's done more for me than any other person I know. He didn't ask me to do this. I volunteered to do it. And he doesn't ask for help often, maybe only once or twice a year."

He relaxed his grip on the steering wheel. "So that's what you meant when you said you couldn't feel me."

She blushed. "Yes. You're the first person I could touch in ten years without instantly knowing your thoughts."

She looked down at her hands for a moment. "That's why I touched you so much in the forest. It's been so long since I had touched another person that I, well, I went a little too far. It was inappropriate, and I'm sorry."

He glanced at her. She hugged Lupe again as the dog stared happily out the windshield, his tongue lolling from his mouth.

"It's just humans you can feel, not animals?" He had a sinking feeling about why she couldn't feel him.

"No, I can feel animals too - dogs anyway. I haven't tried it with cats or other animals. It's different, though, from humans. There are no thoughts, just emotions and feelings. And only with the smart ones. Poodles are the easiest to read, but I've never met a lab that wasn't completely blank."

He snorted softly, and she smiled a little. "It's nice to touch them – nearly all dogs are just happy and excited and full of love."

She paused and gave him an almost sheepish look. "I can read Lupe the best of any dog I've touched. He must be very smart. Maybe it's the part wolf?"

"He's full wolf," Jack admitted.

She nodded. "I figured. He loves you very much, you know."

He grunted, and she said earnestly, "It's true. Dog's emotions are less complex than humans. They run through me like waves of colour. If they're nervous or excited, it's red, happiness is green, and love is blue."

"Dogs are colour blind."

She laughed. "I guess their emotions aren't. If I'm touching

47

Lupe and he looks at you, the most wonderful wave of blue floods through me. It's warm and peaceful and so loving. He would die for you – I can feel it radiating from him."

For some reason, this embarrassed him, and he cleared his throat loudly. They were back in the town now. Ray had turned off at the sheriff's office, and Jack drove aimlessly down the small town's main street.

"Take a right at Gordon," she said. "It's about three more blocks."

"You've never met anyone you couldn't feel before?" he asked.

She shook her head. "Not that I'm aware of. Of course, I go out of my way not to touch people so there could be someone else out there."

He turned right on Gordon, and she directed him to take his second left. He drove down a quiet street. The houses were small and spaced far apart, and Amelia's was the last one on the right. He parked in front of her home and shut off the truck.

"Nice place," he said.

She shrugged. "I just rent it. Thank you for helping me tonight, Jack. I need to ask you for one more favour. Please don't tell anyone about my abilities, okay?"

"I won't," he said. "Make sure you clean the marks on your neck with alcohol."

She touched the small holes in her neck, wincing at the feel of the dried blood caked around them. She stared wide-eyed at Jack. "Do you think that thing will come after me again? He said – he threatened that he would be seeing me again."

"He won't be coming after you tonight, and tomorrow, I'll make arrangements to keep you safe," Jack said.

She stared doubtfully at him before saying, "You're sure he won't come after me again tonight?"

"I'm positive," he said. "You're perfectly safe tonight, Amelia. I promise."

"Okay," she said.

He opened his door and jumped out of the truck. Amelia slid across the seat toward his door, and he lifted her out of the truck. She tensed slightly at his touch but relaxed when he let go of her.

Lupe leaped down from the truck and sat beside her feet. Jack frowned. "Lupe, back in the truck."

The wolf whined but didn't move.

"Lupe. Truck – now."

The wolf whined louder and leaned against Amelia.

Jack stared at him and then shrugged. "Fine. You can stay with her."

Amelia looked up at him. "What? Lupe isn't staying with me."

"I don't think you have much of a choice. Don't worry, he's housebroken," Jack said.

"But I don't have any food for him."

"He'll be fine."

"Um, okay, I guess." She glanced at Lupe and started up the sidewalk to her house, Lupe at her heels.

She opened the front door, and Lupe bounded into the house. She paused and looked back at Jack, waving briefly before entering the house and shutting the door behind her.

Jack climbed into the truck and pulled his phone from his pocket. He scrolled through his contacts and then waited patiently as the phone rang.

A deep voice answered on the third ring. "Jack, you bastard – how the hell are you?"

"Not bad. I need a favour," he said.

"Ask, and you shall receive, brother."

"I need you to drive up to Wenton."

"Wenton? Why?" The man's voice rose in surprise.

"I need you to do something for me. It won't take long."

"That's a two-hour drive, man. I've got a date tomorrow night with Sharon."

"You'll be back in time for your date. Drive up here first thing tomorrow morning, and you can be home by late afternoon at the latest. You owe me, Hank."

"Yeah, yeah," Hank grumbled. "You don't need to remind me. I'll be there."

"Thanks. Call me when you get here." Jack ended the call and leaned back in the seat. He put his hand over his eyes and sighed. It would be a long night.

CHAPTER 7

A melia rubbed her forehead and sipped at the steaming cup of coffee. It was just after seven in the morning, and she felt tired and low. Despite Lupe's comforting presence, she had only caught a few broken hours of sleep, and it was full of strange and scary dreams of the vampire intermixed with images of Jack's warm mouth and hard hands.

She reached down and patted Lupe's head. He panted and smiled at her in the way that dogs do, and she gave him an answering smile. He heard the noise before she did, his ears perking up and a low growl in his throat. Before she could panic, the growl turned into a welcoming whine, and his tail swept back and forth. He ran to the front door just as there was a soft knock. She peeked through the peephole, saw Jack standing in the early morning light, and unlocked the door.

"Good morning," he said as Lupe leaped and jumped around his legs like a puppy. "Down, boy."

Lupe quieted at Jack's feet, and Jack gave him a few rough scratches on the top of his head.

"Hi. Come in," she said.

He followed her into the kitchen.

"Would you like some coffee?" she asked, self-consciously pulling at her t-shirt. She suddenly wished she'd at least put some jeans on instead of yoga pants.

"Sure," he said. Her kitchen was small, with light yellow walls and cream coloured cupboards. It seemed even smaller, with Jack sitting at the table.

"Do you take cream or sugar?" she asked.

"Just black is fine." She set the mug down in front of him, and he sipped the strong, dark coffee as she sat beside him.

"How did you sleep?" he asked.

"Okay. Probably not enough sleep, though. You're here early."

"Didn't sleep that well myself, figured I'd take a chance and see if you were awake."

"Are you staying at a motel in town?" she asked.

"Nah, I hadn't booked one. Hadn't planned on spending the night."

"Where did you sleep then?"

"In my truck."

"Your truck?" She stared at him. "Tell me you didn't spend the night in your truck in front of my house."

When he didn't say anything, just continued to stare at her with those warm brown eyes, she pinched the bridge of her nose and breathed deeply.

"Jack, if I had known you were going to sit outside my house like some kind of superhero, you could have stayed in the house. I have a couch."

"It's no big deal." He took another sip of the hot coffee and looked around. "It's a nice house. Did you decorate it yourself?"

"What? Yeah, I did the decorating myself."

"You're good at it. Do you like doing it?"

"Yes. I guess I do." She wanted to touch him again. God, did she want to touch him again, but she couldn't ask him for that. It would make her look weirder than he undoubtedly already thought she was.

He studied her for a moment before saying, "What is it?"

"Nothing," she said.

"It's something. What is it?" He leaned toward her.

Her face red, she said, "Um, would you mind if I touched you again?"

When he didn't say anything, she chanced a look at him and blushed harder at the look in his eyes. "I mean, not like *touch* you, touch you. I want to see if you're still blank to me."

"Touch away," he said.

The hint of heat in his voice brought an even brighter flush to her face, but her desire to touch him overrode her embarrassment, and she reached out with trembling hands. Steeling herself, she closed her eyes and took his hands in her own. Her worry that last night had been some freak temporary thing disappeared when she didn't hear any of Jack's thoughts. She took a deep breath and smiled at Jack.

"Still blank," she said.

She reluctantly let go of his hands and folded them in her lap. There were a few moments of awkward silence, and then she jumped up. "You must be hungry. I can make you some breakfast."

"You don't have to," he said.

"No, I'd like to." She pulled a couple of pans out from the drawer under the stove and set them on the burners. "Eggs and bacon okay?"

"Yep. I can eat just about anything."

Within a few minutes, the smell of cooking bacon filled the kitchen. She was more aware than she should have been of Jack's gaze as she took some eggs from the carton in the fridge and set them on the counter. She grabbed some tongs and turned the bacon, cursing and jerking her hand back when a splatter of grease landed on her hand.

She dropped the piece of bacon she was turning on the floor. Lupe was up in a flash, crunching it down eagerly as she turned on the tap and stuck her hand under the stream of water.

"You okay?" Jack spoke directly behind her, and she jumped like an idiot.

"Yeah." She shut off the water and reached for the dish-towel to dry her hand. "I just burned my hand a bit."

"Let me see." He took her hand in his and pulled away the towel. There was a small red mark on the flesh between her thumb and first finger, and he ran his thumb gently over it.

She shivered. "Sorry. I'm not much of a cook, I'm afraid."

He raised her hand to his mouth and softly kissed the red mark without speaking. She shuddered again. "Thank you."

"My pleasure." He leaned in, and his hot gaze hypnotized her. "You have beautiful eyes, Amelia. Did you know that?"

She shook her head mutely.

"Your mouth is beautiful, too," he said.

She parted her lips, and his nostrils flared. He dipped his head and placed a warm kiss on her mouth. She moaned softly and leaned into him. He put his arm around her waist and pulled her flush against his body. He kissed her deeply and pushed his tongue into her mouth before backing her up against the counter. She pushed against his hard chest, and he leaned back, breaking the kiss.

"I know you want me." He leaned in and inhaled deeply. "I can smell it on you – your need, your want."

He put his hand on her ass and pulled her against him until she could feel his hardness against her belly. "Invite me into your bed, little Amelia, and we can satisfy our craving for each other."

Amelia could barely breathe, and conflicting emotions rocketed through her. She was nervous, but underneath the nerves, there was a strange urge to take his hand and lead him to her bedroom. To let him do whatever he wanted to her - to trust that he could take away that maddening, throbbing ache between her thighs.

He shifted until he pressed more firmly against her, and the feel of his erection sent an undercurrent of fear through her. She had seen him naked in the forest, and she shivered a little at the memory. She knew how it worked when it came to sex, she wasn't completely naive, but the size of his penis and the thought of trying to take that inside of her cooled the desire in her belly.

She took a deep breath and blurted, "I'm sorry, Jack. I've never, I mean, I haven't been able to touch anyone, and so I've never, well...."

He cocked his head at her before abruptly pushing away and stuffing his hands into his pockets. "You're a virgin."

She blushed. "It's not a disease, Jack."

"I know. It's just I never thought...."

"You never thought what?" Surprisingly, anger was washing over her. She moved the bacon to the stove's back burner before cracking the eggs into a second pan. "Why are you so surprised? I was sixteen when the accident happened. At that point, I'd only kissed one boy my entire life."

She threw the eggshells into the garbage and folded her arms across her torso. "Did you think I would sleep with someone knowing I could feel all of their emotions and thoughts and feelings?"

When he didn't reply, she said, "I tried once. I accepted a date from this nice man I met at the grocery store. And at the end of the date, I decided to kiss him. Only it turned out that he wasn't so nice. We kissed, and his thoughts were so nasty and dirty it made me sick to my stomach. If just kissing him made that happen, what do you think it would have been like if I had actually fucked him?"

To her embarrassment, she was almost shouting at Jack.

He held his hands up and said, "You're right. I'm sorry, Amelia. I spoke without thinking."

Feeling ashamed, she said, "Your eggs are done. I'm going to have a quick shower."

She hurried to the bathroom and stripped off her clothes before turning on the shower. She stepped in and let the cool water soothe her burning skin. She was angry, hurt, and confused. How Jack looked when she admitted to being a virgin made her feel like a leper. Like it wasn't embarrassing enough to be twenty-six and a virgin, and worse - to not have a clue how to kiss or touch someone. Until Jack had come along, she'd resigned herself to never being touched or kissed or having sex. Then Jack walked into her life with his warm body and his intoxicating voice and his stupid 'invite me into your bed' demands, and her neat, orderly life was turned completely upside down.

She turned up the hot water and washed her hair and body before shutting off the shower. She towelled dry and rubbed a hand across the steamy mirror. She examined her mouth and her eyes. Jack had said her mouth and eyes were beautiful, but she saw a too-thin upper lip and tired-looking eyes.

It doesn't matter anyway. Now that he knows you're a virgin, he won't touch you with a ten-foot pole.

* * *

JACK GLANCED AT AMELIA. SHE'D BEEN QUIET AND WITHDRAWN when she returned from her shower. When he tried apologizing again, she shook her head and told him not to worry. She had even apologized for her outburst, making him feel even more like an asshole than he already did.

He tried to get her to eat some eggs and bacon, but she refused, giving her share to Lupe and eating some yogurt and strawberries instead. Once she finished, they'd tidied the kitchen and then left for the sheriff's department.

They were only a few blocks from her house when he said, "Amelia, we need to talk about the vampire."

She finally looked at him. She wore jeans and black arm-length gloves with a T-shirt and an open-collared shirt over the T-shirt. The collar adequately hid the two tiny holes in her neck.

"I know you like Ray and trust him, but I don't think we should tell him about the vampire," he said.

She nodded. "Agreed. Honestly, I don't think he would believe us anyway."

"I've been tracking the vampire for a while and have a backstory to cover the murders. If you're okay with it, I'll do the talking, all right?"

She nodded again and rested her hand on Lupe's shoulder. The wolf sat between them, and Jack knew she'd put Lupe in the middle to keep as much distance between them as possible.

He sighed and turned onto the main street of the small town. He had screwed up back at Amelia's house. She thought his discomfort was because she was a virgin. He didn't know how to tell her that he was ashamed of his behaviour with her. He was so rough with her - kissing her, touching her, and practically dry-humping her in the truck. Hell, he'd come close to taking her in the middle of the woods just because she licked his neck. He groaned inwardly, remembering her hesitation, her surprisingly chaste kisses when he had demanded that she kiss him.

All right, what's done is done. You can't change the past.

He needed to ignore his fascination with her, forget the memory of her soft lips on his, and forget the way she moaned when he touched her. He had never deflowered a woman in his life, and he wasn't about to start with someone who barely knew how to kiss a man.

He pulled into the parking lot of the sheriff's office and parked before smiling tentatively at Amelia. "Ready?"

She nodded, and they walked toward the office in the cool sunshine.

CHAPTER 8

A melia pressed a hand against her abdomen. It was just after eleven, and her stomach was rumbling. She and Jack had been at the sheriff's office all morning. Ray and the coroner had gone to the cabin to pick up Julie's body, and after delivering it to the morgue, the sheriff had sat down with both of them in his small, cluttered office.

"Okay, Amelia. Tell me what happened when that man took you from the cabin." He turned on the tape recorder on his desk.

Amelia took a deep breath. "He carried me into the woods. I was struggling and kicking, but he was too strong. Once we were pretty far in, he put me down and threatened me. He said he would hurt me if I tried to get away. Before he could do anything, though, Lupe showed up and chased him away. Then Jack arrived and helped me back to the cabin."

Ray shut the tape recorder off and stared at her. "He touched you then?"

"Through my clothes, but not my bare skin."

Ray glanced at Jack. "Jack, could you give me a minute with Amelia?"

"He knows, Ray," Amelia said.

Surprise crossed Ray's face, but he said, "Are you sure the guy didn't touch you, Amelia? I hate to do this to you, but if he did, then I might be able to get some information on him."

Amelia shook her head. She hated lying to Ray, but she was confident the truth would be harder for him to believe. "He didn't, Ray. I'm sorry."

He took her hand, squeezing it through the glove she wore. "Don't be sorry. It's better for you if he didn't touch you."

Jack leaned forward. "The man who killed Julie is the man I came here to talk to you about. I've been tracking him for months. He's been linked to a string of murders in the city, and we had our suspicions that he left the city two days ago and was travelling this way. Julie's death confirms those suspicions."

"How do you know for sure it's the same killer?" Ray asked.

"He has a unique way of killing his victims. He inserts needles into their neck and drains them of blood." Jack glanced at Amelia.

"Jesus." Ray ran a hand across the back of the neck. "That explains the needle marks on Julie's neck."

"If you don't mind, I'm going to stick around town for a few days and see if I can catch this guy once and for all," Jack said.

"I can assign some of my men to help you," Ray said.

"I appreciate that, but I work better alone. If I need help, I'll take you up on the offer."

"Sure. But I want to know all the details of your case. If I've got some madman running around my town draining people like some goddamn modern-day vampire, I want to know everything. So, start talking."

* * *

AMELIA LEANED BACK IN THE HARD PLASTIC CHAIR AND TRIED not to fidget. She'd left Jack and Ray to their conversation and had been sitting in the office lobby for the last two hours. Lupe whined and rested his head on her knee. She smiled and patted his head. "Not much longer now, Lupe."

She hoped she was right.

Susan smiled at her from behind her desk. "Can I get you a soda, Amelia?"

"No thanks," she said.

She looked up as the bell above the door jingled, and a young man with red hair and freckles walked into the office. Lupe sat up and sniffed the air, but the man didn't notice her or Lupe. Instead, he walked directly to Susan.

"Excuse me, ma'am." He had a soft, pleasant voice.

"How can I help you?" Susan said.

"I need to speak to the Sheriff."

"He's in a meeting, but I can take your name and number and have him call you back."

"Oh no, ma'am. I need to speak to him in person. If you don't mind, I'll sit and wait for him," he said.

"You may be in for a bit of a wait," Susan said.

"That's fine." He walked toward the seats below the window, smiling politely at Amelia. He had a baby face, and his smooth cheeks were covered in a mass of bright freckles. She smiled a little when he stared at Lupe. "Is that a wolf?"

"Hybrid, actually."

The man stared at Lupe and then at her. Amelia had a distinct feeling that he knew precisely what Lupe was, and she gave him a nervous smile. "Don't worry. He's friendly."

The man nodded, but as he moved toward the seat beside her, Lupe growled at him. His hackles were up, and he stared unblinkingly at the redhead.

"Lupe, stop," Amelia said. The wolf's lip curled up and revealed his large, white teeth. He was still growling, a low rumble in his chest that grew steadily louder.

"I'm sorry," Amelia said. "He's not normally like this."

The man shrugged and moved to the seat farthest from her. He sat down with an effortless grace and stared at the closed door to the sheriff's office. Amelia could see through the glass that Jack was on his cell phone with someone. The conversation didn't last very long, and he returned to sitting at the desk with Ray. They were reviewing something on Ray's computer from the looks of it.

Lupe had stopped growling but sat up and stared intently at the man. Amelia stared at the floor, but from the corner of her eye, she could see the young redhead turn his head and casually sniff the air. It reminded her of Jack and Lupe, and she looked directly at him.

The redhead returned her stare, his nostrils flared and a slight frown on his face. He sniffed again and again, like a dog smelling for its supper. He scratched at the beard on his cheeks - it was the exact colour of the hair on his head - and leaned a little closer to Amelia, still inhaling.

As Lupe began his soft growling again, Amelia frowned. She stared intently at him. There was something different about the man, but she couldn't quite put her finger on it. What the hell was different?

His beard.

The redhead absentmindedly ran his hand over his beard as he stared at her. She was positive when he first sat down, he was clean-shaven. She closed her eyes and concentrated. Yes, she was sure of it. She had noticed the freckles on his cheeks.

The man shifted in his chair like he would switch seats, and Lupe growled a warning. Before the young man could move, the door of the office opened. It brought another blast of cold air in as a bear of a man walked through the door. The redhead wrinkled his nose like he had smelled something terrible and shrunk back into his seat.

The large man approached Susan and rested his hands on the counter. They were the size of small hams, and Susan smiled a bit nervously at him. "May I help you?"

"Why yes, you can, pretty lady." The man grinned at her, and Susan blushed like a teenager. "I'm looking for a guy named -"

"Hank!" Jack exited the sheriff's office and slipped past the swinging gate separating the desks and offices from the main lobby.

He hugged Hank, and they clapped each other roughly on the back. Hank and Jack were about the same height, but where Jack was lean with narrow hips and a broad chest, Hank was barrel-shaped. He was thick and broad and walked with a confident swagger that Amelia suspected he no longer noticed.

"Find the place okay?" Jack asked.

Hank nodded. "Yup. Thanks for the directions. Where's that damn mutt of yours?"

Amelia stood up as Lupe rose and walked gracefully toward Hank, tail wagging happily. She followed him over and stood to the side as Hank made a kissing noise. Lupe stood up and put his front paws on the large man's chest. Hank rubbed and petted Lupe's head and throat roughly. "Hello, you ugly old thing. Did you miss your Uncle Hank?"

Lupe nipped playfully at Hank's shirt and then bounded toward Amelia. He slipped around her legs and peered at Hank from behind her thighs.

"Well, who's this then?" Hank smiled at her.

"Hank, this is Amelia," Jack said. "Amelia, this is my brother Hank."

She held out her gloved hand and watched it get swallowed up in his large one. He bent slightly at the waist and placed a kiss on her hand. "It's lovely to meet you, Amelia."

"Knock it off, Hank." Jack tugged Amelia free of Hank's grip. "Amelia and I were just going for lunch. Why don't you join us? We can -"

Jack stopped, and both he and Hank inhaled deeply.

"Do you smell that?" Hank asked, and Jack nodded. They turned around just in time to see the redhead waiting for Ray slip out the door and disappear down the street.

"Who was that?" Jack asked Susan.

"I don't know. He just asked to speak to the sheriff," she said.

Hank held his arm out to Amelia. "Shall we, m'lady?"

She pulled her gloves up a bit, making sure they were snug against her arms, and then gingerly took his arm in her hand. The three of them left the office, Lupe trotting behind them.

* * *

AMELIA PULLED THE COFFEE MUGS FROM THE CUPBOARD. "ARE you sure you can't stay for coffee, Hank?"

Lunch had been interesting. She nearly fell over when Jack gave Hank the details of the night before, including the part about the vampire attacking her. To her surprise, Hank had listened intently without a trace of disbelief. He and Jack had discussed at length the possibility that the vampire had already left her small town. Afterward, Jack drove her home, and Hank followed them.

"Thanks, but I need to get back. I have a hot date tonight." He grinned at her.

Jack cleared his throat. "Before Hank leaves, I was hoping you would do us a favour, Amelia."

"What's that?" she asked.

"I want you to touch Hank."

She backed up against the counter. Her skin turned cold, and nausea flooded through her. "I can't do that, Jack. You know I can't."

"It's important. Hank is, well, like me, and I need to know if he's also blank to you."

Hank frowned. "What are you guys talking about?"

"You said you would keep my secret, Jack," Amelia said.

"I know, and I'm sorry, but I promise you can trust Hank."

"What do you mean, he's like you?" Amelia asked.

Hank looked everywhere but at her, as Jack said. "Touch Hank, and if I'm right about something, I'll explain then. Okay?"

"This is a bad idea," Amelia said, but she stripped off her gloves. She laid them on the counter and approached Hank.

"Are either of you going to tell me what's happening?" Hank asked.

"I will in a minute, Hank. I promise," Jack said. "Just relax and let Amelia take your hands."

Hank shrugged and held out his hands. Amelia stared at them anxiously.

"Just touch him for a minute, Amelia," Jack coaxed.

Hands trembling, Amelia reached out and took Hank's large hands in her own. Hank stiffened immediately, and she stared into his eyes. He started to shake, and after only a minute or so, Amelia wrenched her hands free. Breathing harshly, she took a few steps back as Hank nearly fell into a kitchen chair.

"Jesus Christ." He stared blankly at Amelia. "Who's Richard?"

Amelia moaned and covered her face with her hands. The tears fell in a hot flood, and she tensed when Jack put his arms around her. He was as blank to her as ever, and she leaned into him as he rubbed her back.

"I'm sorry, Amelia. I had to know," he said.

She nodded against his chest and wiped her face with her hands. Still leaning against Jack, she looked at Hank. "I'm sorry, Hank."

"It's okay. I was just – it threw me for a minute."

"Yeah." She laughed shakily. "I have that effect on people."

"What are you?" Hank asked.

Jack guided Amelia to the table and made her sit down. He poured her some coffee and gave it to her. She wrapped her hands around it, warming them against the hot mug as Jack sat beside her.

"She's a psychic. She can hear people's thoughts, see their memories and feel their emotions when she touches them," Jack said.

Hank glanced at Amelia, and she smiled tentatively at him. "Sharon is beautiful."

She had seen two things when she touched Hank – Sharon and, oddly, the full moon. She was tempted to ask him about the moon thing, but his face suggested it would only freak him out more.

Hank swallowed. "Yes, she is."

"I'm blank to her," Jack said. "I thought you might be as well."

There were a few moments of silence, and then Hank stood up. "I should go if I'm going to get back to Sharon in time for our date."

Jack stood with him. "I'll walk you to your car. Amelia, I have a few errands to run, but I'll return in a few hours. Keep your doors locked, and don't open the door to anyone. Lupe will stay with you, okay?"

Amelia nodded, pretending not to notice Hank giving her a wide berth as he passed her in the small kitchen.

"Goodbye, Hank," she said softly. "It was nice to meet you."

"Likewise." Hank gave her a pale grin as he and Jack left the house.

CHAPTER 9

"I'm sorry, Hank. I needed to know if I'm blank to her because of what I am," Jack said as they stood beside Hank's car.

Hank ran a still-shaking hand over his face. "You could have warned me, Jack."

"I thought it would be better if you didn't know," Jack replied. "What does it feel like when she touches you?"

Hank shuddered. "I don't know how to explain it. It's terrible. It's like she's rifling through your brain, picking through your emotions and thoughts, and you can't hide anything from her. And then, you start feeling *her* thoughts and almost all of them center on this Richard guy."

He paused. "And you."

Jack ran his hand through his hair. "What about me?"

Hank looked acutely uncomfortable. "Let's just say I know exactly how much she wants you – in horrifying detail."

Jack blushed, and Hank chuckled. "You always did have a way with the ladies, little brother."

"I need you to do me a favour." Jack pulled a small

notepad from the back pocket of his jeans. He ripped off the top sheet with two names scribbled on the lined paper. "These are the names of Amelia's parents. Can you research and find out what you can about them?"

Hank nodded and stuffed the piece of paper into his pocket. "How did you get their names?"

"I asked the sheriff for them. I told him that I might be able to help Amelia with her problem."

Hank arched his eyebrow. "And he believed you? I don't think there's a cure for this type of thing."

Jack shrugged. "He cares deeply for Amelia and desperately wants her to be happy. He was easy to convince that there might be something we could do to help her."

"What do you think her parents' background will tell you?"

"I don't know, but it's a start, right?"

Hank nodded. "I'll call you as soon as I have some information."

"Thanks, Hank. I appreciate that. Don't say anything about Amelia, okay? Not even to Sharon."

"I won't say anything."

"Good." Jack fished in his pocket for his keys. "I'm going back to the woods to see if I can pick up the bloodsucker's trail. I've got his scent from the clothes Amelia wore the night he attacked her."

"You're going hunting?" Hank's light brown eyes suddenly glowed with a fierce light. "Perhaps I should join you."

Jack laughed. "You want to risk Sharon's wrath?"

The light faded in Hank's eyes. "Yeah, you're right. If I miss our date tonight, she'll have *my* head on a pole. Just promise me you'll be careful, Jack."

"I always am."

* * *

AMELIA MOANED IN HER SLEEP BEFORE WHISPERING, "Richard?"

Tears dripped down her cheeks, and Lupe, lying on the floor beside the couch, whimpered softly. He licked her hand consolingly, but she was deep in the throes of her nightmare and didn't wake.

"I'm sorry, Richard," she muttered. She was back in the wreckage of the car, her leg pinned and throbbing. She stared at Richard's face and waited for the darkness to blot out the vision of Richard's pale, dead face. Instead of the darkness she expected, Richard's eyes opened, and he stared at her.

"It should have been you, Amelia," he whispered. Blood suddenly burst from his mouth, spraying her with its solid warmth.

Amelia shrieked piercingly, Richard's words horrifying her more than the blood soaking into her skin. She screamed again as a familiar voice invaded her dream.

"Amelia, wake up."

She clawed her way out of the dream toward Jack's voice, opening her eyes to see Jack staring worriedly at her. Shaking and gasping, she allowed him to sit her up on the couch. When he sat beside her, she curled into him, wrapping her arm around his waist and burying her face in his shoulder.

"You're okay. It's fine. Everything's fine," he said.

Still shaking, she forced herself to move away from Jack's hard body. "What time is it?"

"Just after dinner. You fell asleep," Jack said.

"How did you get in here? I locked the door."

He shrugged a little sheepishly. "I took your keys when I left."

71

She knew she should be angry with him but was just grateful for his presence. She went willingly when he put his arm around her and urged her against him. She curled up to his warm body, shifting until she could tuck her face against his neck.

"Are you okay?" His deep voice rumbled above her.

"Yeah. Just - bad dreams."

"Do you want to talk about it?"

She shook her head. "No."

"Okay." He was quiet for a bit, his hand rubbing her back while Lupe stared silently at them from his spot on the floor.

"Jack, I -"

"Amelia, I'm sorry I -"

They both stopped, and she sat up, staring into his face and smiling a little. "Go ahead."

"I wanted to apologize for earlier."

"It's okay. Touching Hank wasn't that terrible. I could tell he's a good person."

"No, I mean I want to apologize for this morning and yesterday in my truck."

She turned bright red as he said, "I've made you believe that I think your virginity is a bad thing."

"Jack, I do not want to talk about this." Amelia was blushing so hard she was nearly sweating.

"Please," he said. "When you told me you were a virgin, I reacted badly, and I'm sorry for that. I want you to know that I reacted badly because I was so," he paused, his tanned face reddening a little, "rough with you. If I had known you were that inexperienced, I wouldn't have said or done the things I did."

"Oh my God," Amelia groaned. "This is mortifying."

"There's nothing to be embarrassed about, Amelia." When she didn't reply, he said, "Seriously, you shouldn't be embarrassed by this."

"Oh really?" Anger flickered in her veins. "I'm twenty-six years old, and not only have I never had sex, but I also don't have a clue how even to kiss or touch a man. I kissed a boy as a teenager, and a decade later, I kissed you. And we both know how well I did that."

He stared at her thoughtfully. "Why don't you practice on me?"

"What?"

He smiled, a warm, inviting grin that made her stomach do flip-flops. "You can practice on me."

"Jack, it's not – I mean, I can't just start kissing you," she said.

He shrugged. "Sure you can. I'm the perfect person to practice on. You know that."

"What do I need to practice for? I have a feeling people who are blank to me are pretty rare," she said sullenly.

He shrugged again. "If you've found one, you'll find more. And when you do, do you want the same thing to happen? I don't mind taking one for the team."

She could feel her cheeks burning. "I don't need your pity kissing, Jack."

He laughed and pulled her onto his lap. "It's not pity kissing, Amelia. I've been dying to kiss you all day. I'm fascinated with your mouth."

"Yeah, right," she said. Shamefully, just the feel of his thighs under hers was heating her up, bringing that aching throb to her core again.

He laughed again and slid one large hand around the back of her neck. He tugged her face towards his until she could feel his warm breath on her mouth. "Kiss me, Amelia."

"I'm not sure – I don't know…."

"Like this." He placed a soft kiss on her mouth, and she shivered in his arms.

"Your turn," he said.

She kissed him tentatively and then again when he made a small sound of encouragement.

After a few moments, he licked her bottom lip with the tip of his tongue. "Open your mouth, Amelia."

Trembling, she did as he asked, and he licked both her upper and lower lip before sliding his tongue between them. He explored her mouth leisurely, his hands rubbing her upper arms, and when he finally stopped, she was panting and flushed.

"Now you," he encouraged and then kissed her again. Hesitantly, she slipped her tongue into the warm recess of his mouth, feeling the smoothness of his teeth before their tongues met. They kissed hungrily, tongue sliding against tongue as their breathing quickened and Jack's hands slipped from her arms to her back. He pulled her up against his body until her breasts were pressed against his firm chest. He sucked hard on her tongue, making her whimper with pleasure, and then slid his hands under her t-shirt. He ran his hands up and down her back, tracing circles on her soft skin with his fingertips.

She tugged shyly at his shirt, and he helped her pull it off. She stared at his chest, fascinated again by the smoothness of his skin and the hair that covered it. Tentatively, she leaned forward and placed a soft kiss in the hollow of his throat. Encouraged by his low groan, she kissed his throat again, this time with an open mouth and an exploring tongue. He shuddered and gripped the back of her head in one large hand as she moved down his throat, licking and sucking. When she reached the juncture of his neck and shoulder, she paused and then nipped him experimentally. He shuddered again, a muttered plea slipping from his lips, and she smiled before licking the spot where she had nipped him.

As she kissed his neck and chest, she ran her hands down over his rib cage and across his flat abdomen. His skin radiated heat, and he moaned and gripped her tightly as she explored him with her mouth and tongue. After a moment, she angled her mouth over his, thrusting her tongue into his mouth with new confidence. He met it with his own, holding her head and kissing her deeply.

His hands pulled impatiently at the hem of her t-shirt, and, after a moment's hesitation, she lifted her arms so he could pull it over her head. She was wearing a pale blue bra, and he leaned forward and kissed the tops of her breasts.

She moaned and clutched at his head as he licked his way up to her collarbone, tracing it with the tip of his tongue. He stroked her soft skin while his lips skimmed the delicate column of her throat. He cupped one breast in his hand, running his thumb over the nipple before moving his hands to her back. His hands had released the clasp of her bra before she knew what was happening. Her bra loosened, and she tensed. She clamped her arms to her side to keep her bra in place and gave him a worried look.

"If you want to stop, we can." He kissed her again gently – just soft presses of his lips against hers.

"I don't want to stop – not yet," she said and returned his kiss, sliding her tongue between his lips.

Was kissing someone always like this, she wondered inwardly. Just the feel of Jack's tongue stroking hers brought wave after wave of pleasure through her body. When his fingers grasped the straps of her bra and tugged gently, she relaxed her arms so that he could pull the bra free of her body. He tossed it to the floor and stared appreciatively at her naked breasts. She crossed her arms over them, and he frowned before gently pulling down her arms.

He looked up at her, and she blushed furiously at the look in his eyes. He cupped one bare breast, both of them moaning a little at the contact. He ran his thumb over her rose-coloured nipple, his nostrils flaring when it immediately hardened and pinched it lightly between his finger and thumb. She gasped, and with a low groan, he moved her until she was lying on the couch. He pushed her thighs apart and settled his body between them. She could feel him hard and heavy against her, but before she could become nervous, he was kissing her again, kneading and cupping her breast with one hand.

He traced the outline of her ear with his tongue and then sucked on the lobe while he plucked gently at her hardened nipple and rolled it between his fingers. Just as she was wondering what it would be like to have his mouth on her breast, he dipped his head and captured one nipple between his lips. He sucked hard on the rosy peak, and she cried out loudly, her hips thrusting involuntarily against him. He licked and sucked and nibbled on both nipples until she was crying out and writhing beneath him. Each tug of his mouth sent a spasm of pleasure straight to her belly, and she clutched his head in her hands, feeling like she was drowning.

The area between her thighs was aching with such intensity that Amelia could hardly breathe. Boldly, she moved her hand to the waistband of his jeans and slipped her fingers beneath it. He grabbed her hand and yanked it free.

"Stop," he rasped against her breast.

Embarrassed to her core, she stared at him. "I'm sorry."

He shook his head. "No, don't be. It's just – if you touch me like that, I won't be able to stop."

"Maybe we don't have to stop."

"No. You don't want your first time to be with someone like me."

She frowned. "What do you mean?"

"It's not important. Just trust me on this, okay?"

She tried to kiss him again, and he sat up with a sigh of

regret. "I think that's enough for one night, Amelia. I'm sorry. I shouldn't have let it go as far as it did."

Amelia sat up and reached for her t-shirt on the floor. She pulled it on awkwardly and sat on the edge of the couch, her hands tucked between her knees and her face burning. Her face burned brighter at the memory of what they had done. She had made a fool of herself.

"Amelia?" He touched her shoulder tentatively, and she pulled away. "I'm sorry, really I am. This was a bad idea."

"Was I that terrible? Christ, I'm embarrassed." She rubbed her hand over her face.

"No, that's not it. I just didn't think I would -"

She held her hand up. "Forget it, Jack. I appreciate you taking one for the team, but I didn't sleep well last night and am exhausted. I think I'll call it a night."

"Amelia, wait," he said.

"If you don't mind sleeping on the couch, you and Lupe are welcome to spend the night. I'll grab you some blankets and a pillow. There's plenty of food in the fridge. Help yourself." Without looking at him, she hurried out of the living room.

CHAPTER 10

Amelia woke to a gloved hand across her mouth.
Before she could struggle, his other hand wrapped around her throat, and a voice breathed, "I can crush your windpipe easily. Do you believe that?"

She nodded, and the pressure eased around her throat.

"Good. Don't move or make a sound," he whispered.

There was the soft purr of tape ripping, and duct tape was placed firmly on her mouth. He threw back the covers and pulled her into a sitting position before holding her hands in front of her and wrapping her wrists tightly with more duct tape.

The clock beside her bed said it was just past midnight, but bright moonlight flooded through her open window, and she could see the face of her attacker. It was the young man who had looked at her so strangely at the sheriff's office earlier this afternoon. Although a black knitted cap covered his red hair, the freckles on his face stood out in stark relief.

He wore a long-sleeved black hoodie, jeans, and leather gloves covering his hands. She stared at him with a mixture of terror and confusion as he swung her legs out of the bed until she sat on the edge.

He leaned in and stared at her, his face only inches from hers. "There's someone who wants to meet you. I'm carrying you out the window, and you won't struggle. Do you understand?"

She nodded and glanced at the closed bedroom door. She briefly wondered how long it would take Jack to discover she was missing. She eyed the nightstand beside her bed. If she could kick it over and make some noise, Jack might be able to get to her in time.

The redhead followed her gaze and grabbed her chin. "I'll kill him. Do you want that?"

She shook her head no, her eyes wide and terrified. With a quiet grunt, he heaved her over his shoulder. She winced as his shoulder poked painfully into her rib cage. Her arms and hands, still taped together, hung down to his lower back. His hoodie had ridden up, and she could see a band of pale flesh just above the waistband of his jeans. As he carried her toward the window, she steeled herself and rested her hands against his bare skin.

He froze, and Amelia, her eyes squeezed shut, screamed behind the duct tape. Images rushed through her head - a snarling pack of wolves working together to take down a frightened deer, a man with a long scar across his chest crouching naked on the ground, his skin rippling and his body changing. A gigantic wolf snarling and snapping as, with one swipe of its paw, it tore off the head of the vampire who had fed from her.

She moaned, tears leaking down her cheeks as an image of the bright, full moon flooded through her. She could feel how it called to him, how he couldn't resist its hypnotic pull, and at that moment, it also called to her. A voice echoed through her head.

Eric, my sweet. Come to your mama. Don't you be a bad boy now. Come to your mama.

With a soft roar, the man threw her across the room. She crashed into the wall, wincing as her head bounced off of it, and landed in a crumpled heap on the floor. Vaguely, she was aware of Lupe barking and Jack running through the house.

Her assailant shook and shuddered violently. As she watched, he lifted his head and let loose with a half-howl, half-snarl. Her eyes widened in horror as the man's body swelled and his face sprouted hair. His clothes exploded from his body, and he transformed into a red wolf. He crouched down, snarling and grinning at her with his long, white teeth. He stepped toward her as her bedroom door flew open, and Jack burst into the room. He wore just a pair of jeans, and she screamed again, the sound muffled by the tape, trying to warn him as the wolf spun around and growled at him.

Jack made his own howl of rage, and she watched in shock as he transformed into the wolf she had seen in the forest. He was much larger than the other wolf, and as he stalked toward her kidnapper, snapping his teeth, the red wolf leaped for the open window. With a short howl, Jack chased after it. As the wolf bounded through the window, Jack latched onto his back, his sharp teeth sinking through the thick pelt and into the soft flesh underneath it. The wolf screamed and twisted toward Jack, his claws digging at the window frame. With a yowl more suited to a cat, he snapped at Jack's face. Yelping, Jack released the wolf, blood flowing down the thick fur on his face.

The smaller wolf squirmed through the window and disappeared into the night, howling loudly. The neighbourhood dogs responded with a chorus of barking. When Lupe went to jump out the window, Jack barked once. Lupe immediately flattened to the floor, staring up at the larger wolf with clear adoration.

Jack turned and padded toward her. She shrank back as he approached, and his green eyes glowed softly. His head was larger than hers, and as he eased forward and sniffed delicately at her face, Amelia moaned quietly beneath the duct tape plastered over her mouth. He made a soft chuffing noise, blowing her hair from her face, and she closed her eyes.

"Amelia?"

She opened her eyes. Jack crouched before her, naked with blood oozing from a wound above his eye but back to his human form.

"Hold still, honey. This is going to hurt." He pulled the duct tape quickly from her mouth, frowning at her small cry. "You okay?"

She nodded, and he worked to remove the duct tape from around her wrists as Lupe sat beside her and licked her face consolingly.

"Lupe, stop." Lupe eyed Jack and then quickly gave her one last lick.

Jack rolled his eyes. "Damn dog. Ever since he met you, he doesn't listen for shit."

She smiled weakly at him as he removed the last of the duct tape. He helped her to her feet, steadying her when she swayed a little.

"Here, you need to sit down." He tried to lead her to her bed, but she shook her head.

"You're bleeding."

He touched the wound on his forehead, his fingers coming away bloody. "I'll be fine."

"Come with me." She took his hand and led him to the bathroom. "Sit down."

She closed the lid to the toilet, and he sat down after

wrapping a towel from the rack around his waist. She opened the medicine cabinet and reached for the peroxide and a package of gauze. Her hand shook badly, and she stared at it for a moment, willing it to stop trembling. After a few seconds, it obeyed, and she took a deep breath and opened the bottle of peroxide. She soaked the gauze with the cold liquid and dabbed delicately at the wound. He winced, and she murmured an apology.

The wound was already starting to clot, and she cleaned the smears of blood around it before holding a towel below it and pouring half the bottle of peroxide over it. It bubbled and foamed, and she rinsed it several times before blotting it dry. She pulled out a box of bandages from the cabinet under the sink, along with a roll of white hospital tape, and set them on the sink.

He smiled a little. "You're well prepared."

She carefully applied the bandage to his head. "I don't like hospitals. You're going to need stitches. This will do until you can get to the hospital."

"I won't need to go to the hospital. I'm a quick healer."

She gave him a look of exasperation. "You'll still need stitches."

"I promise you I won't." He stood and reached for her. She stepped back, staring cautiously at him.

"I'm not going to hurt you, Amelia. I want to check you over, make sure you're not hurt."

"I'm fine."

"Let me check," he insisted.

She stood still as he ran his hand over her scalp, checking for bumps or scratches. He ran his hands quickly and efficiently over her body, and although there was nothing sexual in his touch, she could feel warmth starting in the pit of her belly. Ashamed and confused by her reaction, she pushed away his hands. "Enough. Please."

"Amelia, I -"

"It's your turn now, Jack. What are you?"

"Come to the kitchen. I'll make you some tea and explain."

* * *

ANTHONY STOOD NAKED AT THE WINDOW, STARING OUT INTO the darkness. He heard his mate, Leah, stirring in the bed behind him. She padded softly across the floor and wrapped her arms around his torso.

"The bed is cold without you," she said.

"He should be back by now." He continued to look out the window.

"He's fine. Eric isn't a child – he can take care of himself." She pressed her warm nakedness against him. "He probably decided to hunt after his errand."

Anthony frowned. "He better not have. David told him specifically to get the information and come straight back."

Leah slipped to his side and placed one hand on his cheek, tilting his head down to face her. "You can't protect him forever. He's old enough to make his own choices."

She traced the long, twisting scar from his collarbone to his hip bone. "Come back to bed."

"In a little bit."

She sighed and hugged him briefly. "I'll see you soon."

Thirty minutes later, he caught movement in the clearing. Eric moved slowly across the clearing, bent at the waist with one hand pressed against his back. Throwing on a pair of pants, Anthony opened the door and slipped out into the cool night air.

Anthony met him in the middle of the clearing. "Eric, what happened?"

"Anthony," Eric groaned and collapsed. Panic making his

heart thud heavily, Anthony heaved Eric over his shoulder and carried him into the cabin.

"Leah! Eric is hurt." He carried Eric into the second bedroom and dropped him carefully on the bed. Leah entered the room, wrapping her robe around her body and turning on the light.

Blood pooled under Eric's body, and Leah helped Anthony turn him over. She pulled up his sweatshirt. "He's been bitten, and it's deep. Go to the bathroom and get some towels. And grab the first aid kit under the sink."

When Anthony didn't move, she slapped him lightly on his bare chest. "Honey – go now!"

CHAPTER 11

J ack set the cup of tea in front of Amelia. He wore a pair of shorts but hadn't bothered with a shirt. He was impressed by how steady her hand was when she brought the cup to her mouth and took a small sip.

"Amelia, there are…." He honestly wasn't sure how to continue. He didn't like the idea that she might be afraid of him now.

Amelia set her cup down. "You're a werewolf."

"Not exactly. We call ourselves Lycans, and our kind has existed for thousands of years."

"That man in my bedroom," she shuddered a little, "I touched his skin, and I could feel his thoughts. The moon – it called to him, Jack. It was the same with Hank. He… holy shit, Hank's a werewolf too."

"Lycan," he corrected.

"That's what you meant by being the same as you. You thought Hank would be blank to me because he's also a werewo–Lycan."

He nodded, and she rubbed her forehead wearily. "You changed tonight, you both did, but it's not a full moon."

He pulled out the chair and sat down across from her. "We don't need the moon to be full to shift. We can shift from human to wolf and back whenever we choose. Well," he paused, "the adults can. Our children are more sensitive to the moon's cycle and are helpless to stop the shift when it's full."

He reached forward and took one of her hands in his. She flinched a little and then relaxed. He hoped it was from years of avoiding contact with people and not because of what she had seen earlier.

"The world is full of paranormal beings. That vampire that attacked you - Lycans – that's just the tip of the iceberg. Paranormals are far greater in kind than humans. It's just that, for the most part, we avoid humans. We keep to our kind, or we keep the true us hidden."

"That vampire who attacked me? He wasn't keeping to his kind."

"Vampires are different. They're," he grimaced, "soulless and depraved and fight like dogs amongst themselves. They need humans to survive, but they don't kill them for the most part. Not out of any sense of honour or compassion, just to keep their food source available. They usually stick to the larger cities where the humans are plentiful, and vampires blend in. To find one this far out in the country is extremely uncommon."

She shivered again, and he squeezed her hand. "Don't worry about the leech that attacked you. I have his scent, and it's only a matter of time before I find him. He'll never touch you again. I promise you that."

"He's already dead," she said.

Surprise crossed his face. "How do you know that?"

"The Lycan that tried to kidnap me – when I touched him, one of the things I saw was a wolf ripping the head off of that vampire. He was an enormous wolf." She hesitated. "Bigger than you."

"He must be the leader of the group you have here," he said.

"We have a group of Lycans living in our town?" Disbelief coloured her voice.

He smiled at her. "Unlike vampires, most Lycans prefer the countryside."

"Why did that Lycan come to my home?" she asked. "He said there was someone who wanted to meet me. What could they possibly want with me?"

"Honestly, I'm not sure. But I intend to find out."

She swallowed. "If you bit me, would I turn into a Lycan?"

He stared gravely at her. "Yes, if it was the full moon. A Lycan's bite will only turn you if it happens during the full moon."

She shuddered a little, and he squeezed her hand. "That rarely happens. Please believe me, Amelia. We Lycans prefer to have as little contact with humans as possible."

He gave her a small smile. "Lycans who have integrated themselves into the real world, Lycans like Hank and me, are rare. I promise you that. I can't even remember the last time a Lycan infected a human."

"Why are you and Hank so integrated?" she asked.

Getting into Lycan history was the last thing he wanted to do, but he couldn't deny her an answer. Besides, there was a part of him that wanted her to know.

Maybe it would help her understand why he couldn't be with her.

Maybe it would help remind him why he couldn't be with her.

"Lycans live in packs," he said. "These packs are large, extended families. They live together, hunt together, look out for each other and build a community, you know? Each pack has its own rules regarding how they interact with humans. Some packs forbid any type of contact. Others are more lenient. But no matter how willing they are to deal with humans, Lycans generally don't mate with them. And they are discouraged, if not outright forbidden, to marry or have children with them."

She frowned. "Why?"

"Many Lycans feel it weakens the bloodlines. If a half-breed even can shift, which plenty of them don't, usually they don't have as much control over their wolf sides. It can be dangerous to have a half-breed running around, unable to stop themselves from attacking pets and farm animals or even humans. Full-blooded Lycans feel that humans are inferior and that a Lycan who mates with a human is weak."

"So Lycans are a bunch of bigots?" She asked, her voice so full of indignation that he grinned.

"We're not all like that. Even back then, there were Lycans marrying humans. It was just more secretive. A half-breed can be taught to control their wolf side just as well as a full-blooded Lycan can. It just takes more time and effort. There's been a major shift in the last twenty years in how Lycans view humans. They realize that living together in harmony is better than segregating themselves."

He stood and filled her cup with more tea, setting it down in front of her before retaking his seat. She nodded her thanks and took a sip of the steaming liquid as he continued. "My father was a Lycan who strongly believed we needed to live peacefully with humans. So much so that he fell in love with a human woman and married her. Unfortunately, the pack he belonged to didn't share his philosophies, and shortly after my mother discovered she was pregnant, they were kicked out of the pack."

"That's awful," she said.

"My father took a job working nights as a janitor. I grew up happy and loved. I had no idea how much my father missed the pack and how much he had sacrificed for my mother and me. I didn't even know what I was. My parents had never spoken of the Lycans, and my father never turned in front of me. They thought it was better not to say anything until they knew that I would shift. Most Lycan pups turn before their second year, and I was already eight years old and had yet to shift. I suspect that my father believed I never would.

"Where are your parents now?" Amelia asked.

Even after all this time, sorrow coated him in a thick layer. "At that point in time, the Lycans and the vampires were in the middle of a war. Ten years ago, a truce of sorts was declared., although there are reports of individual vampires and Lycans being killed by each other. But back then, there was no peace between our kinds. Vampires discovered my father was a Lycan, living without his pack, and one night, they attacked us in our home. It was late. I was sleeping, and my mother came into my room, pulled me from my bed and hid me in the closet under a pile of blankets. She told me to stay where I was no matter what happened, and then she kissed me and left."

He shuddered, and Amelia squeezed his hand. "I remember being afraid, and I remember my mother screaming. The attack, adrenaline, and fear it brought on prompted my first shift. I was terrified. The first few times you shift, it's painful and disorienting, and I had no idea what was happening. The neighbours heard the screaming and called the police, but they arrived too late. Both my parents were dead."

"I'm so sorry, Jack," she said.

"The first officer on the scene found me in the closet. I was shifting back and forth from human to wolf, unable to control it, screaming and thrashing in the blankets. This man, Tom, immediately knew what I was."

He smiled a small and bitter smile. "I got lucky that night. Tom not only knew what I was and how to help me, but he was a human who had married a Lycan. Tom and his wife Joy applied to be my foster parents. Two years after that, they officially adopted me. Joy explained to me what I was, and she taught me, along with their son Hank - a half-breed - how to hunt, control the shift, and live among the humans without our true natures being revealed. Both Hank and I decided to join the police force. Mom and Dad live in the suburbs outside of the city. Dad's retired and spends most of his time puttering in his garden. They have the small house and the white picket fence and couldn't be happier."

He paused and rolled his eyes. "Well, other than grand-children. They've been pestering Hank and me to give them some for years."

She smiled a little. "Did you ever -"

She stopped, and he raised his eyebrows encouragingly. After a few seconds, she said, "Did you ever have any contact with your birth father's pack?"

He stood and stared moodily out the small window above the sink. "I had no idea where the pack was, but Joy found them for me. She was still in contact with some of her old pack members, and they helped her find my father's pack. When I was in my teens, I joined them briefly. It didn't go well. They didn't trust me because I was a half-breed. After a month, I went back to my family."

She stood beside him at the sink, emptying and rinsing her cup. She stared up at him, and he gave her a small smile.

"Are you okay? It's a lot to process, I know."

She nodded. "Actually, yeah, I am. It's comforting to know that I'm not the only different one."

He laughed a little, and she grinned at him. He reached

out and ran his fingers through her hair. "Are you sure you aren't hurt from earlier?"

"I'm fine," she said. She moved closer to him, and this time, Jack took a step back only to be blocked by the counter.

"Amelia, it's late."

She nodded and reached upward, brushing her fingers across the bandage on his forehead. "Does that hurt?"

He shook his head no, and she stepped closer until the tips of her breasts touched his chest. He groaned under his breath as she cupped the back of his neck with one small hand and urged him to bend until his face was only inches from hers.

"Thank you, Jack." He could feel her warm breath on his lips, and it took all his willpower not to kiss her. "Thank you for saving my life tonight and in the forest yesterday."

"You're welcome," he said.

She brushed her lips against his, and when he didn't protest, she kissed him again, this time probing gently at his closed mouth with her tongue. He opened his mouth with a low moan and allowed her to explore his with increasing urgency. Unable to stop himself, he sucked gently on her tongue until she gripped the back of his neck.

She stared shyly at him. "I want you to share my bed tonight, Jack."

He stood quietly for a moment with his eyes closed and his nostrils flaring before he looked down at her with regret. "That's not a good idea, Amelia."

"You don't want me." She stepped back, a look of shame and hurt crossing her face.

"That's not it," he said dryly. "Trust me."

"Then what?" She frowned at him. "I know you've slept with human women before. This morning, you were more than willing to share my bed. It's because I'm a virgin, isn't it?"

He paused, groping for the right way to say it before finally admitting it. "Yes."

She flushed again, her cheeks bright red, and a look of anger flashed across her face. "You're doing a bang-up job of convincing me that my virginity isn't a bad thing, Jack."

She stepped away from him and tried to leave the kitchen, but he took her arm and pulled her to a gentle stop.

"Let go of me, Jack," she warned.

"Not until you hear me out. Please, Amelia."

She yanked her arm free and crossed them over her chest. "I'm listening."

"The thing is – Lycans aren't known for their gentleness. Do you understand what I'm saying?"

She nodded sullenly, and he frowned. "I don't want to hurt you. You're little and fragile, and just taking your virginity will cause you pain. Your inexperience and me being a Lycan means the possibility of hurting you is high."

She rolled her eyes. "That's a ridiculous excuse, Jack. Before you knew I was a virgin, you were more than willing to take me to bed, and I'm not little. I'm 5'10, for God's sake."

"You think you want this with me, but trust me, you don't," he said.

"Don't tell me what I want. You barely know me."

"That's my point. I'm the first person you've met since your accident that you can touch. We're attracted to each other - it's natural to think sleeping with me is the right thing to do. But it isn't. You'll find a human, someone normal, that you can touch. I can't be the only one out there," he said.

"And if you are?" she asked.

"I'm not." He rubbed a hand across his face wearily. "Amelia, listen to me. It's not that I don't want you. You know that I do. But even before I found out you were a virgin, it was a mistake for me to touch you the way I did. It's just that

Lycans have an excellent sense of smell, and I can smell how much you want me. It overrode my common sense, and I made a mistake in -"

"So, this is my fault?" She arched one eyebrow at him. "Because I smell?"

"No," he said, frustration making the word hard. "That isn't what I meant. I just mean that your scent is very intoxicating, and it's hard to resist the -"

Looking defeated and bone-tired, Amelia held up her hand. "I get it, okay? I'm exhausted, it's been a long night, and I think I'll return to bed."

He frowned. "I'm not explaining myself very well."

She shook her head. "Seriously, Jack. It's fine. Now that the vampire is dead, you'll leave in the morning anyway. I'll try to keep my smell to a minimum until then."

"I'm not leaving until I find out why that Lycan tried to kidnap you," he said.

Acting like she hadn't heard him, she left the kitchen.

He went into the living room and collapsed on the couch, staring miserably at Lupe. "Could I have fucked that up anymore?" He squinted at the wolf, who licked his hand in commiseration.

He stared blankly at the wall across from him. What he had said to Amelia wasn't a lie - he was deathly afraid of hurting her. He had been with human women before, but they were always equal to him in experience and had no trouble handling his occasional roughness. In fact, human women were all he had been with. He hadn't met a Lycan female yet who was willing to mate with a half-breed, and the human women he slept with had no idea he was half-Lycan and would have run screaming if they had.

If he was truly honest with himself, it wasn't just his fear of hurting her that held him back. Amelia's willingness to mate with him, even after seeing him in wolf form and knowing that he was a half-breed, was disconcerting. He had never met anyone like her. When he burst into her room to see her crumpled on the floor with a Lycan about to attack her, Jack had been overwhelmed by the fear that rushed through him.

With a harsh sigh, he lay down on the couch. His feet hung over the edge, and it was too narrow for him to lie on his back, but he pulled the blanket to his chest and closed his eyes. He could stay in a motel but wasn't about to leave Amelia alone and vulnerable. Not until he found out what the Lycans wanted from her.

CHAPTER 12

A soft murmuring woke Jack. He sat up on the couch, wincing and rubbing at the kink in his neck and stared around blearily. Lupe was nowhere to be found, and he could hear the soft sound of Amelia's voice.

He glanced at his watch. It was just after eight, and he stretched before standing and following the sound of her voice. There was a small room just down the hallway from the kitchen, and he peeked through the half-open door to see Amelia sitting at a small desk. She had a headset on, and he could see the soft glow of the computer screen in front of her.

"Okay, and tell me what it says now?" She cocked her head as she listened, one hand scratching absently at Lupe's head as he sat next to her with his head in her lap.

"Perfect. I want you to move your mouse to the 'C Drive' folder and click twice. Good. Now, click on the 'Program Files' folder."

Lupe spied Jack and made a soft 'woof' in greeting. Amelia glanced behind her and nodded at him, holding her hand up in a five-minute gesture.

He nodded and left her with Lupe, using the washroom, before returning to the kitchen. A half-full pot of coffee was warming on the coffee maker, and he hunted through the cupboards until he found a coffee mug. He poured himself a cup and sat at the table, sipping cautiously at the hot liquid.

Lupe bounded into the kitchen, nudging his arm affectionately and wagging his tail as Amelia trailed in after him.

"Good morning, Jack." She poured herself another cup of coffee. She added a generous dollop of milk and sat at the table across from him. "How did you sleep?"

"Good," he lied.

"Sure, you did," she said.

He laughed. "Your couch is a little small, but it was better than the front seat of my truck. What were you doing in there?"

"Working. I'm employed by a small firm that provides online computer assistance for people."

It made sense that she would have a job where she didn't interact with people in person. "Do you enjoy it?"

She shrugged. "It pays the bills."

She took another sip of coffee and stared at the bandage on his head. "How's your head this morning?"

He touched the bandage that he'd completely forgotten about. "I'm sure it's fine."

She stood up. "Let me look at it. You'll probably need to go to the clinic this morning and get stitches."

"It's fine. Lycans have -"

"Hush," she said as she stood before him and reached for the bandage. He relented and let her peel away the tape. She pulled back the bandage and gasped softly in surprise.

"What the hell?" She ran her fingers lightly over his skin. "The cut is completely gone."

"Lycans heal quickly. I told you I wouldn't need stitches." He grinned at her as she looked down at him.

"That's incredible." She touched his skin again, running her fingers over the flesh. "I've never seen anything like it."

He leaned back a little. Her touch affected him in a way that he wanted desperately to avoid, and she blushed and moved back to her chair.

"Sorry."

"It's fine," he said more gruffly than he intended.

Looking embarrassed, she said, "So, do you ever get sick with a cold or the flu?"

"No. Some half-breeds do. They lean more toward the human side and can contract illnesses or human diseases. Their healing powers aren't nearly as strong, and they can be killed by something other than silver or another Lycan."

She bit her lip. "So that's not just in the movies. Only a silver bullet can kill a Lycan."

"A full-blooded Lycan," he corrected. "With half-breeds, there's no guarantee."

"But if you don't get sick and you heal that easily, the odds are high that only silver could kill you, right?" she asked.

He shrugged. "I don't know. There's only one way to find out, and I'm not keen on experimenting."

She nodded and stood, brushing nervously at the front of her jeans. "I'm having breakfast, and then I need to return to work. Would you like something?"

"You don't have to make me breakfast. I can make myself something or grab something at a restaurant."

"Don't be silly. I have plenty of food." She moved to the cupboards and opened one of the top ones. She stretched upward, reaching for the cereal box on the top shelf.

"I have cereal. There's oatmeal. I could make eggs and bacon again. Whatever you -"

Anger washed over him, and he stood and silently crossed

the kitchen to touch the smooth skin on her side where her shirt had ridden up.

She jumped, giving him a surprised look. "Jack? What are you doing?"

"He hurt you." His voice was low, almost a growl, and he heard her breath catch in her throat. He had no doubt that his eyes were now green and glowing and that a thick beard had grown on his jaw. He could barely contain his anger at what the Lycan had done to her.

He lifted her shirt higher, and she looked down at the bruise that had blossomed on her hip like a dark flower. He tugged down the waistband of her jeans, exposing more of the bruise, and touched it with his warm hand.

"I must have gotten it when he threw me against the wall." She pushed his hand away, a blush rising up her neck.

He stood silently, his hands curled into tight fists, as a low growling started deep within his chest. Lupe stood and stalked forward on stiff legs. The hair on his neck stood up, and he growled in response to Jack.

"Jack? You're... you're getting bigger."

His biceps bulged, his shirt straining at the sleeves.

"Jack? Calm down." She spoke softly, soothingly. He stared at the bruise, and she pulled down her shirt, hiding it from his view.

"I'll kill him for hurting you," he growled.

"It doesn't hurt," she said. "I just bruise easily." She cupped his face hesitantly, her fingers stroking his beard. "Relax, okay?"

He sucked in a harsh breath and closed his eyes, willing his wolf to retreat. With a low snarl, it obeyed. He shook himself roughly, staring around blankly for a moment as Lupe settled onto his haunches beside him, and she dropped her hand back to her side.

"I'm sorry. I didn't mean to frighten you," he said.

"You didn't frighten me."

He instinctively knew she had told the truth. She wasn't afraid of him, even if she stood in her kitchen with a Lycan who apparently didn't have control over his shifting quite how he thought he did.

"I don't normally lose control like that," he said hoarsely. He staggered back and leaned against the counter, rubbing his hand across his face. "I don't know what happened."

"You're tired, Jack. You need more sleep," she said.

"Lycans don't need much sleep. I'm fine."

"You've gone forty-eight hours with hardly any sleep. Why don't you crawl into my bed for a few hours?"

He glanced at her, and she blushed bright red. "I need to get back to work, so it's not like I'll be using it."

He paused, tempted to get uninterrupted sleep in a real bed, and then shook his head. "No, I'd better not. I need to talk to Ray again and do some investigating into the Lycans that are living here."

She sighed irritably. "Ray won't be at work today. He's off on Fridays. Get some more sleep, and I'll wake you up for lunch."

He opened his mouth to argue again, watched her face set in a stubborn scowl, and nodded. "Okay, you win. I'll sleep for a few hours."

She gave a small cat-like smile of satisfaction as he pushed away from the counter and headed for her bedroom. He paused at the doorway and looked back at her. "Don't leave the house without me, Amelia. Not until I know what the Lycans want from you. Do you understand?"

She nodded, and he left the kitchen and walked towards her bedroom. Her soft voice followed him down the hallway. "Lupe puppy, do you want some bacon? Does my good baby boy want some crunchy bacon?"

He smiled as he entered her bedroom. He stripped off his

clothes, letting them land on the floor because he was too tired to pick them up. He crawled between the sheets, laying his head on the pillow and inhaled deeply. Her scent, a combination of lavender and vanilla, was all over her bed, and he found it oddly soothing.

* * *

"How's he doing?" Anthony asked as Leah left the guest room.

"He's better this morning." She smiled reassuringly and dropped a kiss onto the top of his head. "The wound is healing, and his fever is gone."

"Is he awake?"

"Off and on. He needs to rest, though." Leah began to make coffee in their small kitchen.

"I need to speak to him before David does."

Leah glanced back at him. "Maria stopped by while you were in the shower. David is gone again."

"Goddammit!" Anthony stomped to the front closet. He pulled his jacket on with quick, jerky movements. "He's losing his mind, Leah."

She glanced around nervously. "Anthony, hush."

He joined her in the kitchen, taking the cup of coffee she handed him. "Everyone knows it. How long are we going to pretend it's not happening? We can't have him leading the pack any longer. He's too unpredictable, too volatile. This is the third time he's just disappeared into the forest this month. What the hell is he doing out there?"

She shook her head. "I don't know. But talk like this will get you killed. You don't go against the pack leader, Anthony. Martin chose David to lead, remember?"

"I remember. I also remember that it was seventeen years ago, and David still had all of his goddamn marbles."

Leah took a small sip of her coffee. "What would you have the pack do then? David can be unseated as a leader only if he dies or another Lycan challenges him and wins. There's a reason no other Lycan has challenged him in his nearly twenty-year reign. No one can defeat him."

"So, we just let him lead us into danger? Risk exposing our true nature to the town? They already think us strange for living way the hell out in the woods, to begin with."

She smiled a little. "They think we're ignorant inbred hill-billies. And that's exactly what we want them to think. They keep their distance, and we keep ours. That's the way it's always been, Anthony."

"But what if it didn't have to be that way?" Anthony set his cup down. "What if we could live among the humans? They don't have to know what we are. Other packs have tried and succeeded at it. It's happening more and more frequently. Look how many Lycans have mated with humans. Hell, I bet there are more half-breeds than there are full-bloods now."

Leah smiled sadly at him and ran her hand over his fore-head. "I know, my love. But David would never allow us to leave the forest. I'm surprised he even lets us work and shop among the humans. You know how he is."

Anthony snorted. "David is clinging to the old ways. His insistence on segregating ourselves from the humans and his impending madness will get us all killed eventually."

Leah frowned. "He's suddenly taken an interest in humans."

"One human," he corrected. "That's another thing – what is with his obsession with this woman? This Amelia? For someone so hell-bent on keeping us away from the humans, he certainly is anxious to get his hands on her. He's going insane, and the pack will have to deal with it sooner or later."

Leah stared at him. "My love, you need to be careful what you say and who you say it to. Many are loyal to David."

"Perhaps not as many as you think, Leah."

She started to ask him what he meant, but he pulled her against him and captured her mouth in a rough kiss.

"I need to go to work," he said against her mouth. "I will speak with Eric when I return tonight."

He paused and then kissed her again, this one slow and thorough. "I love you, Leah."

"I love you too, Anthony."

CHAPTER 13

J ack woke with a start. The sunlight slanted through the window, casting warmth and shadows on the wall. He glanced at the clock next to the bed. It was after two, and he threw back the covers and sat naked on the side of the bed.

He listened carefully, satisfied when he could hear the soft murmur of Amelia's voice even through the closed bedroom door. She was still working, and although he was dismayed at how long he had slept, he couldn't deny that he felt better, stronger, and more like himself.

He stretched and padded to the bathroom. Amelia had brought his overnight bag from the living room and placed it on a small stool outside the bathroom door. He hadn't intended to stay for longer than a night and brought only one change of clothes. He would have to ask Amelia if he could use her washing machine.

He smiled when he realized that at some point while he was sleeping, she had gathered up his dirty clothes and washed and dried them. They were folded and placed carefully on the stool under his bag, and he was grateful for her thoughtfulness. He snagged his toiletries bag out of the overnight bag as he entered the bathroom and quickly brushed his teeth before turning on the shower. She had placed a large, folded bath towel on the side of the sink, and he draped it on the towel rack before stepping under the warm spray.

* * *

AMELIA PULLED OFF THE HEADSET AND TILTED HER HEAD TO the left and right, stretching her neck's stiff muscles. She could hear the shower and knew that Jack had finally woken. She debated waking him up at noon, and had crept into her bedroom, and stared silently at his sleeping form. He was lying on his back, the sheet and quilt low on his hips, and sleeping deeply.

She had stared at him with unabashed delight, enjoying the opportunity to look at him without feeling the need to hide it. She had watched his broad chest rising and falling with slow, even breaths, admiring the dark hair that covered it and how it narrowed into a thin, perfect line below his navel. She felt a nearly childish sense of delight at having a man sleeping in her bed. A bed she believed would only ever be used by her.

Holding her breath, she took a few steps closer until she stood beside the bed. She stared for a long time at the spot where the sheet stopped above his pelvis. She wondered if he would wake if she took a quick peek under the sheets. Over the last day, her mind repeatedly wandered to that moment in the woods when she saw him naked. He had looked so huge to her, and she wondered, not for the first time, how it would feel to have him inside her.

He told her he was rough. Although she suspected he told her that to frighten her, it only increased her curiosity and desire if she was honest. What exactly did he mean by rough? He'd been gentle when they were making out on the couch. She shivered a little at the memory of him lying between her thighs, of his mouth pulling on her nipples and his hands stroking her skin. Despite her rapidly growing desire for him, a tingle of fear went down her spine when she thought of the moment in the forest again. His penis had seemed very large to her, but it was the first one she had seen in person. Maybe he was average. Maybe he wasn't nearly as large as she thought. She had been frightened and woozy from blood loss after all.

It wouldn't hurt to take a quick look. Just to see if it is as large as you remember.

Her hand had been reaching for the sheet when her common sense kicked in, and she pulled her trembling fingers away from him. Her pulse thudding rapidly in her ears, and her entire body shaking, she'd quickly gathered up his dirty clothes and fled the room. She was acting like some horny schoolgirl, and, away from the profoundly appealing vision of Jack's naked chest, she was mortified by what she'd nearly done. Jack had been clear he wouldn't sleep with her, and she just needed to accept it. She was only embarrassing herself with her repeated attempts to convince him otherwise.

Sighing deeply, she stood and smiled down at the wolf at her feet. "C'mon, puppy. Let's see if I can find you something other than bacon to eat."

* * *

FRESHLY SHOWERED AND DRESSED, JACK REACHED FOR HIS CELL

phone when it buzzed loudly. He sat on the side of Amelia's bed and answered it. "Hank, what's going on?"

"Hello to you too, Jack," Hank said.

"How was your date with Sharon?" Jack grinned into the phone.

"It was lovely, thank you," he answered almost primly. "Listen, I have some information about Amelia's parents."

"That was quick."

"Slow day at the office," Hank said.

"What have you found out?"

"Amelia's adopted."

"You're kidding me," Jack said.

"She and her twin brother Richard were adopted by Laura and Walter Barlow when they were a month old."

"Are you sure?"

"I'm positive. The records are well-hidden, but you'll find them if you dig deep enough. It was a private adoption, but Amelia's parents are from her hometown. By today's standards, Laura and Walter paid a modest fee to adopt her and her brother, and no documents on record state her actual parents' names."

"Holy shit."

"Yeah. Does Amelia know?"

Jack stood and walked to the window, staring blankly at the street. "I don't know. If I had to guess, I would say no, but that's not something people share with strangers. I'll have to ask her."

"Ask me what?"

Jack glanced behind him to see Amelia standing in her bedroom doorway. "Hank, I have to go. Thanks for your help."

"Later, little brother." Hank ended the call.

Jack shoved his phone into his pocket and stared at Amelia for a moment.

"Ask me what, Jack?"

"Amelia, are you still in contact with your parents?"

She frowned. "Once a month, I have a very awkward dinner with them. Why?"

"I got your parents' names from Ray and asked Hank to investigate."

She gave him a guarded look. "Why would you do that?"

"I thought it might help us determine why you have your gift."

"It's a curse," she said.

"I thought there might be something in your parents' past that would help shed some light on why you are the way you are."

"And? Did Hank find anything?" she asked.

"He did," he said cautiously.

"What did he find?"

"Amelia, you're adopted," he said.

She jerked in surprise. "I'm not adopted."

"You are, honey. Both you and Richard were adopted by your parents when you were a month old. Hank found the adoption paperwork."

"He's wrong. There's no way Richard and I were adopted. I mean, my parents – they would have told us. They wouldn't have kept something like that from us. My mom talked about being pregnant with us. She had horrible morning sickness, and Dad couldn't cook meat in the house the whole time she was pregnant with us. He has to be wrong."

"He's not, honey," he said.

"Did he… did the papers say who our real parents are?"

"No, they didn't. But it doesn't mean we can't find out. They're from here. He knows that much. We just need to dig a little -"

She turned abruptly and left the room. He chased after her. "Amelia, what are you doing?"

She had already thrown on a sweater and pulled a pair of gloves from the front closet. "I'm going to talk to my parents."

"Wait – let's have a bite to eat and talk this over first. You can speak with your parents after dinner."

"I've lost my appetite. You're welcome to whatever is in the fridge. I'll be back in a few hours."

He shoved his feet into his boots as she pulled on her sneakers and grabbed her car keys. "Nope. You're not going anywhere alone. I'll drive you to your parents."

"It's fine. You don't need to be a part of my family drama. They don't live far from me, and I won't be gone long."

She reached for the door handle, and he took her arm. "Amelia, just wait a minute."

"Let go of me, Jack!" She tried to wrench her arm free and balled her hands into tight fists when he refused to let go. "Let me go – I mean it!"

She looked up at him, her face angry and her eyes bright with unshed tears before her sudden fury deflated like a balloon. The tears slid down her cheeks, and he pulled her into his arms. She rested her head against his chest and wiped at the tears on her cheeks.

"I need to go and see them right now," she said.

"I know. Let me go with you, okay?"

She hesitated and then nodded. "Okay."

* * *

"Amelia, what are you doing here?" Amelia's mother was petite, blonde, and chubby, with fine lines around her eyes and mouth. She clutched at the edges of her cardigan and peered at Amelia and Jack.

"Is that a wolf?" Her eyes dropped to Lupe, panting softly at Jack's side.

"Mom, this is my friend Jack and his dog, Lupe. Jack, this is my mom, Laura. Can we come in?" Amelia's hands shook, and she chewed at her bottom lip. She looked up at Jack when he took her gloved hand in his warm one and squeezed encouragingly.

Her mother nodded, glancing at their entwined hands before stepping back to let them into the house.

"Your father is still at work, but he should be home soon," she said as they walked into the kitchen. "I haven't even started dinner – I thought you were coming by next week."

"I'm not here for dinner." Amelia sat at the kitchen table, and Jack sat beside her. Her fingers traced the table's worn wood as Lupe rested his head on her lap and stared at her.

"Oh." Her mother paced around the room. Her daughter clearly made her nervous, and Jack reached for Amelia's hand again as her mother gave him a quick look.

"Would you like a glass of water? A cup of coffee? I think I have some iced tea." She started for the fridge.

"Mom - sit down for a minute, please. We need to talk."

"What do we need to talk about?" Her mother hesitated and then slid into the chair farthest from Amelia. Her hands twisted in her lap as she stared at them.

Amelia leaned forward, and her mother shrank back a little. "I need to ask you something, and you need to be completely honest with me. Okay?"

She frowned. "Of course, dear."

"Were Richard and I adopted?"

Her mother immediately paled, the colour draining from her face like someone had pulled a plug, and Jack was sure she was going to faint. He jumped up and crouched beside the woman, touching her arm.

"Laura," he said, "take some deep breaths."

Amelia crouched on her other side, placing one gloved hand on her other arm. "Mom? Do you need to lie down?"

"No," she whispered. "Could you get me a glass of water?"

Amelia poured her a glass of water as Jack returned to his chair. He sat on the edge of it, ready to jump up and catch the woman if she suddenly passed out. She was taking deep breaths as he had instructed, and as Amelia handed her the glass of water, she smiled faintly.

"I'm sorry," she said.

Amelia returned to her seat, petting Lupe's head absently when he whined and shoved his head back into her lap.

"Answer the question, please, Mom."

Her mother drank water and set the glass back on the table. It chattered briefly against the wood, and she stared at her shaking hands. "We should wait until your father gets home."

"Mom." Amelia reached out, ignoring the way her mother flinched, and rested her gloved hand against her mother's hand. "Tell me the truth. Were Richard and I adopted?"

"Yes," Laura said.

Amelia sat back in her chair like she'd been shot. She stared mutely at her mother as Lupe whined again and nudged her leg.

"Lupe, enough," Jack said, and the dog quieted.

"Why didn't you tell us?" Amelia asked.

"We were going to." Her mother's face was a cottage cheese white. "I swear we were going to tell you when you were teenagers, but there never seemed to be the right time, and as far as your father and I were concerned, you *were* our biological children."

"You lied to us," Amelia said. "You told us stories about being pregnant with us."

Her mother flushed. "I'm so sorry. I shouldn't have done that. It's just that we tried for so long to have children, and then we found out that I could never carry a child to full term. We were devastated, but then we got the chance to adopt you and your brother. The day we brought you both home was the happiest day of our lives. I guess I just wanted you to be mine so badly that I, well, I made up memories of being pregnant with you."

"You should have told us!" Amelia shouted.

"We were going to!" Tears leaked down Laura's cheeks. "Your father and I had decided that we were going to tell you, and then – then Richard died, and you changed. You weren't the same, Amelia."

She took a deep breath, the tears dripping steadily down her face. "You changed. You became distant and withdrawn, and you wouldn't let us touch you anymore. I was afraid if we told you then that you were adopted, we would lose you completely."

She reached for Amelia's hands, holding them firmly and stroking the back of them through the leather gloves. "My child had just died. I couldn't stand the thought of losing the other one, too. Do you understand that?"

"You wished that Richard had lived," Amelia said dully, staring at their clasped hands. "After the accident, you hugged me, and I knew - I *knew* - that you wished I had been the one who died and that Richard had lived."

Her mother made a harsh sob. "No, Amelia! I would never wish for that."

Amelia pulled her hands free. "It doesn't matter now. Richard's the one who died, and I turned into a freak."

Her mother swiped at the tears running down her face. "What do you mean?"

"It doesn't matter what I mean." She stared at her mother. "I want to know who my birth parents are."

"Amelia, we should wait for your father. I'll make dinner, and we can sit and talk about this. He can help explain why -"

"No!" Amelia shouted and slammed her fist down on the table. Her mother made a small moaning sound, and Jack took Amelia's fist in his hand. He worked her fingers apart, kneading her hand through the soft leather of the glove until it relaxed in his grip.

"I don't want to wait for Dad," she said. "I want to know who my birth parents are, and I want to know now."

Laura stared at her, her mouth trembling and tears still sliding down her cheeks. She reached for the pad of paper and pen sitting on the far end of the table. She wrote down a name and address, ripped the paper from the pad, and slid it across the table towards Amelia.

"We kept in touch over the years. I sent her pictures of you and Richard and wrote her letters about how you were doing."

Amelia glanced at the address before tucking it into the pocket of her jeans. She stood up, and her mother stared up at her. "Where are you going?"

"I want to talk to this woman," Amelia said.

"Amelia, wait. Please – could you wait until your father gets home? The three of us could meet with her together," Laura said.

Amelia shook her head. "No. I want to meet her on my own."

She reached for Jack's hand, and he stood and walked with her to the front door. Her mother trailed after them. As Amelia started down the steps, her mother called her name, and they turned back to look at her.

"I'm sorry, Amelia. I really am. Will you – are you going to come by for dinner next week?" Her mother gave her a look of helpless bewilderment.

Despite what they'd just learned, Jack could smell Amelia's love for her adoptive mother radiating out of her.

"Yes, I'll be there for dinner. I'll call you and Dad in a few days, okay?"

Her mother nodded eagerly, the tears on her face glinting in the cold sunlight. "Okay. I love you, Amelia. Both your dad and I do – very much."

"I know, and I love you too. Give Dad my love. I'll call you."

CHAPTER 14

"Amelia, are you okay?" Jack stared worriedly at her.

She nodded and continued picking at the plate of food before her.

After leaving her parents' home, they'd driven to her birth mother's house. It was just outside of town, a small hobby farm with a large vegetable garden in the side yard and a tiny barn with a fenced-in area behind the farmhouse. Two horses were grazing in the fenced area, and they'd looked up curiously when Amelia knocked loudly on the farmhouse's front door.

Jack could already tell there was no one home. The place was quiet and still. No cars were parked in the driveway, and he didn't catch any human scent. After she'd knocked a few times without any answer, Jack cupped her elbow and steered her back toward his truck.

"We'll try again tomorrow," he said as he lifted her into the truck.

She'd stared listlessly out the window as he drove back to town. At her insistence, he stopped at a pet store and picked up some dry food for Lupe. She'd agreed when he suggested picking up take-out, waiting patiently in the truck with Lupe while he ran into the town's only Chinese food restaurant and picked up some food.

Now, Jack watched as she stabbed at a piece of broccoli with her fork and dragged it to the other side of her plate. She had hardly eaten anything, and he frowned when she pushed away from the table.

"Amelia, you haven't eaten enough."

"I'm not that hungry. I'll eat more tomorrow," she said. "I think I'll have a bath. It's been a long day. You could watch TV, or there are some books on the bookshelf in the living room."

"Okay." He began to clear the plates from the table, and when she started to help, he said, "Go have your bath. I'll clean up."

She nodded and rubbed at her forehead before disappearing down the hallway. Lupe watched her go and looked at Jack, whining softly.

"Go on then," he said.

Lupe padded silently after her. As Jack scraped her uneaten food into the garbage and began loading the dishwasher, he heard the tub filling and Amelia moving about her bedroom. She was completely silent. In just a few short days, he had grown used to her soft chatter to Lupe, and her quietness unnerved him. He bitterly wished he had never asked Hank to investigate her parents' background.

* * *

JACK HESITATED, LISTENING TO THE SOFT SOUNDS OF AMELIA behind her bedroom door before he knocked lightly.

"Come in."

Jack opened the door and poked his head in. He stared silently at her for a moment, taking in her damp and flushed cheeks, the tiny droplets of water sliding down her bare arms and legs, and how the robe she wore draped her body. She had pulled her hair up into a messy bun, and he could see drops of water clinging to the dark strands of hair.

She pulled nervously at the front edges of her robe, tucking them more securely around her, and he groaned inwardly as the fabric highlighted the curves of her full breasts. He could remember exactly how her nipples had tasted, and it took all of his willpower not to cross the room and kiss her.

"Are you going to bed?" His voice was too loud in the quiet, making her jump a little.

"I thought I might," she said. "I know it's early, but I'm tired and have a bit of a headache."

"That's fine. I just wanted to check your window." He moved across the room and confirmed that it was locked securely.

"What if someone comes back again tonight?" she asked.

"I'll be surprised if they do. Keep your bedroom door open, and if you hear any noise, go into the bathroom and lock the door. Lupe will stay in your room tonight. He'll alert me if there's any danger."

"You could stay in my room." She stared steadily at him. "The bed's big enough for both of us, and you won't get any sleep on the couch, you know that."

Her bed was a small double, and he had no trouble picturing how easy it would be to stretch out next to Amelia's warm body. There would be no way to avoid touching her in the night. He had a clear vision of him leading her to the bed and stripping off her clothing. He would kiss her and touch her soft flesh until she was moaning and crying out for him, and then he would tuck her under him, part her thighs and make her his.

"Jack?"

He realized he was gripping the windowsill so tightly his knuckles were white. "That's not a good idea, Amelia."

She flushed with embarrassment. "What if I swear I won't touch you?"

She raised her right hand, her tone bitter when she said, "I solemnly swear the horny virgin will keep her hands off you all night."

"It's not you that I don't trust."

She dropped her hand, and shame and confusion crossed her face. "I'm sorry, Jack. It's been a hard day, but I shouldn't be taking it out on you."

"It's fine. Lupe will stay in the room with you. If there's anything suspicious, he'll let us know."

He walked to the door of her bedroom and paused in the doorway. "Good night, Amelia."

"Good night, Jack."

* * *

JACK WOKE TO THE SOUND OF LUPE GROWLING SOFTLY. HE HAD fallen asleep sitting on the couch, and he was on his feet and moving toward Amelia's room instantly. He entered the room silently, his heart stopping at the sight of Amelia's empty bed before his gaze landed on her standing at the window. Lupe was beside her with his hackles raised, staring intently out the window, growling softly and continuously.

Jack joined them at the window. "You're supposed to be in the bathroom with the door locked."

"Something or someone is moving outside, I think," she said.

He searched the darkness of her small backyard, letting his breath out in a harsh rush when he saw the creature scurrying across the far end of her yard.

"It's a raccoon." He petted the top of Lupe's head. "Quiet, Lupe."

"A raccoon?" She frowned and leaned closer to the window. "How can you tell? It's completely dark out there."

"Lycans have excellent night vision."

"Oh, right. Of course." She stepped back from the window, shivering and rubbing her arms.

Jack stared down at her. She wore a plain, white cotton nightgown that clung to her breasts and barely covered her ass. He stared at her long, pale legs as his mouth went dry. He swallowed and took a step towards her.

"Jack? Are you okay?"

"Fine," he muttered thickly. "I like your nightgown."

She looked down at herself in confusion, her face reddening a little.

"It's just cotton," she said as he took another step towards her.

"I like cotton," he said. He clenched his hands into fists and closed his eyes, breathing shallowly and trying to control his urge to pull Amelia into his arms and kiss her. The smell of her desire was thick in the room, and both her need and his own chipped away at his self-control.

You'll hurt her. Do you want to do that to her?

He opened his eyes to see her staring up at him, her cheeks flushed and her mouth trembling. He looked at the lovely, pale column of her throat. The two tiny pinpricks from the vampire's bite were almost completely healed now.

She took a step closer, bridging the final gap between them, and as her scent washed over him, he was lost. He groaned and dipped his head, placing a soft kiss at the base of her throat. He could feel her pulse fluttering rapidly like the wings of a frightened bird beneath his lips, and he trailed a path of warm kisses up to her ear.

"You invited me into your bed last night, and I said no," he said. "Will you invite me again?"

"Yes," she breathed. "I want you in my bed, Jack."

He cupped the back of her neck and kissed her. She opened her mouth, and he slid his tongue in, tasting and licking at her tongue as she moaned and pressed her body against his. He didn't have to take her virginity. He could just take her to bed and make her come. He would show her how good it could feel, and maybe, if he were lucky, she'd be willing to touch him and bring him pleasure as well.

It would be better that way. There would be no fear of hurting her, and her first time could be with a human, someone normal who she could spend the rest of her life with. There was bound to be a human out there who was blank to her. His stomach clenched painfully at the thought of another man touching her, but he pushed the thought out of his head and pulled her body up against his.

She moaned into his mouth and tugged at his shirt impatiently. He pulled it off and tossed it to the floor before undoing his jeans and pushing them down his legs. He caught a glimpse of fear on her face, but he kept his boxers on and pulled her back into his arms.

"Anytime you want to stop, just tell me, and I will," he said.

She looked at him solemnly. "I don't want to stop. I'm just a little nervous."

He kissed her again as he cupped her ass and kneaded it lightly. When he released her mouth, she made a soft cry of disapproval and rubbed herself against him. He reached for the hem of her nightgown, curling his fingers around the edge of the fabric. She raised her arms, and he swept it over her head. She wore a pair of pink boy shorts beneath it and reddened a little at his small grin.

"I don't have any, uh, sexier underwear."

"You don't need sexy underwear." He grinned at her. "They'll just be pulled off anyway."

She blushed fiercely at his words, and he laughed and picked her up, carrying her over to the bed and easing her down. He knelt over her for a moment, staring down at her smooth and pale body until she was squirming a little.

"Jack," she said and held out her hand.

He stretched out beside her. He nudged her legs apart and pushed one hard thigh between them before running his hand up her ribcage and cupping her breast. He ran his thumb over her nipple, smiling against her throat when it hardened immediately, and she arched her back in silent supplication.

He kissed her again, their tongues tangling together as she thrust her hips against him repeatedly. He plucked roughly on her nipple, and she gasped into his mouth, her fingers digging into his back. He kissed his way down her throat and to her collarbone. He used the tip of his tongue to trace a slow, meandering path along her collarbone and to her shoulder before nipping it lightly.

Her moans spurring him on, Jack bent his head and captured one hard nipple between his lips. She arched her back again and clutched at his head. He teased her nipple with his lips, tongue, and teeth before switching to her other breast. He sucked on her nipple until it hardened in his mouth and then pulled gently on it with his teeth.

"Oh my God!" Amelia's soft cries were making his cock drip. She pulled on his head until he lifted it and then shoved her mouth onto his. He kept still, letting her explore his mouth with her tongue until she pulled away, gasping and moaning.

"Please, Jack," she panted.

"What?" he said into her ear before sucking on her earlobe.

"Please, I need – I mean, I want - I don't know!" she said.

He could almost taste her frustration and her need, and it went straight to his dick, spilling fresh precum out of the tip.

He trailed his fingers down her abdomen, stopping to circle her navel before slipping his hand inside her panties. He traced small circles in her soft curls before sliding his fingers between her wet and swollen lips. He rubbed gently at her clit, making it swell under his fingers. She cried out and bucked her hips against his hand, her fingers digging into his back. She moaned and repeatedly gasped as his fingers circled and rubbed and pressed.

Jack stared down at Amelia. Her face was flushed, and her mouth was swollen from his kisses. With a low groan, he moved his hand and slid one finger deep inside of her. She gasped softly and opened her eyes, staring up at him. He smiled at her and placed a gentle kiss on her mouth before sliding his fingers back to her clit and circling it lightly.

"Oh, Jack," she panted. Her legs fell open, and she thrust her pelvis against his hand as small gasps and moans escaped from her mouth. He watched as she suddenly grew quiet. Her body stiffened under him before she let out a loud cry, and a surge of wetness flooded his fingers.

She twitched and shook under him, her eyes squeezed shut and her breath exploding from her lungs in short, hard gasps. He kissed her forehead, cheeks, and the tip of her nose before capturing her mouth. He sucked gently on her lower lip, and she wrapped her arms around his shoulders and pulled him down against her.

"Oh my God, Jack," she muttered against his throat. He ignored the throbbing of his cock and smiled at her, brushing her hair away from her face.

"That was incredible." She smiled shyly at him. "Thank you."

He laughed. "You're welcome."

She stared at him briefly, biting her lip nervously, and then slid her hand over his chest. She rubbed her fingers through the hair before letting her thumb drift across his flat nipple. He inhaled sharply when she slipped her hand down his abdomen, touching the hard muscles there before she traced the thin trail of hair below his navel. He put his hand over hers when she tried to slide her hand into his boxers.

"You need to stop, Amelia."

She scowled. "Why?"

"Because you have no idea how you affect me. If you touch me, I...." He trailed off, trying to choose his words carefully.

"Oh no, you don't, Jack." Her scowl deepened. "We are not stopping now."

* * *

AMELIA DIDN'T CARE WHAT JACK SAID. SHE WASN'T LEAVING him unsatisfied when he'd just given her an amazing orgasm. She pulled her hand free of his and slipped it inside his briefs. She reached for his cock, wrapping her fingers around him and smiling smugly at his low moan.

"Fuck, Amelia," he groaned.

She stroked him experimentally, watching as his eyes closed with pleasure and he pushed his hips into her hand. She rubbed and squeezed slowly, marvelling at how warm he was. She stroked her thumb over the tip, a little surprised by the amount of moisture that had gathered there, as he reached up and cupped her breast, kneading it roughly.

Suddenly anxious to see him, she pulled impatiently at the waistband of his briefs. He lifted his hips and pushed them down his legs, kicking them off his feet before settling onto his back. She relaxed next to him and stared at his cock with shameless curiosity.

It was as large as she remembered, and she stroked him lightly with the tips of her fingers, liking the way he groaned and squirmed under her hand. She held him firmly and moved her hand up and down the shaft, varying the strength of her grip and the speed of her hand movement. He seemed to swell even more in her hand, and she was a little surprised at how hard his cock was beneath the velvety soft skin.

She glanced up at his face. His eyes were closed, and he was panting lightly, his hips moving with the rhythm of her hand. Her gaze returned to his cock, and she was struck by the sudden urge to taste him. She wondered briefly if that would be considered too forward, but she decided she didn't care and bent over him. She slid her mouth over the tip of his cock, tasting the slightly salty moisture on her tongue, and made a muffled gasp of surprise when he cried out and thrust his hips upwards, sliding his cock deeper into her mouth.

"Oh Christ," he groaned when she slid her mouth back to the head of his cock and sucked experimentally.

She licked the head of his cock and was secretly pleased with the way it made him shiver and moan. Curious about how much of him she could fit in her mouth, she opened her mouth wide and slid her lips down his cock.

With a loud curse, he grabbed her shoulders and pushed her away. She stared at him wide-eyed, afraid she had done something wrong. "I'm sorry, Jack."

He sat up and pushed her roughly onto her back. She squeaked in surprise when he yanked her underwear down her legs. He threw them to the floor before grabbing her thighs with his hard hands and pushing them apart. He settled his body between her thighs and kissed her hard, shoving his tongue into her mouth while he rubbed and cupped her breasts. He rolled her nipple between his thumb and finger before pinching it lightly, and she moaned against his mouth.

"Don't be sorry. You have no idea how much I want you," he muttered hoarsely.

"I want you too, Jack. Please." She kissed his jaw, trailing her tongue over his rough skin before nipping at his earlobe. She wasn't lying. Despite her recent orgasm, the slow cycle of heat had started up in her belly again, and she moved her hips in a gentle rolling motion against him. His cock slipped across her wetness, and they both gasped in response.

"I don't have any condoms," he suddenly groaned.

"I'm on the pill," she said.

"Lycans, even the half-breeds, do not get STIs," he said.

She smiled at him and pressed her hips against him once more. "Then don't stop, Jack."

"Your first time shouldn't be with someone like me," he protested, but even as he spoke, he was reaching between them, grasping his cock, and guiding it to her warm, wet slit.

"Yes, it should. I want you to be my first." She smiled at him and kissed him slowly, urging his mouth open so she could slide her tongue in.

"Don't make me beg," she breathed against his mouth, and he made a soft, strangled noise in the back of his throat before pushing the head of his cock into her.

She gasped, and he stopped immediately. "Amelia, have I hurt you?"

She shook her head. "No. Don't stop."

He pushed a little further into her before stopping again when her thighs squeezed his hips.

"Okay?"

She nodded and pushed her hips lightly against him. She wanted this, wanted it desperately, but she could feel her body stiffening in anticipation of the pain. She took a few deep breaths and tried to relax her body, but her legs were beginning to tremble around him. He had barely entered her, and already she felt stretched and full.

"Are you sure about this?" he asked.

She nodded. He kissed her, coaxing her mouth open and sliding his tongue against hers. He rubbed her bare hip, circling and tracing her soft skin without moving deeper into her.

As Jack kissed and touched her so gently, Amelia could feel her nervousness subsiding. He kissed her until her fear and tension had completely melted away. He pushed fully into her with one smooth movement when she relaxed beneath him. Amelia tore her mouth from his and cried out. It hurt more than she imagined it would, and she took a few deep breaths as Jack stared down at her.

"Are you okay, honey?" Jack asked.

"Yes. Just give me a minute."

"I'm sorry." He kissed the tip of her nose and then her lips gently. "We can stop."

He tried to move off of her, and she clung to him.

"No, I don't want to stop. Kiss me, please," she said.

He bent his head and kissed her slowly, sucking on her lower lip before tracing her upper lip with the tip of his tongue. She took his hand and guided it to her breast. He cupped the warm, pale globe and teased her nipple until it was a hardened point.

Amelia moved under him, tensing and waiting for the pain. There was pain, but this time, it was dull and faded quickly. Jack stared anxiously at her, but when she moved again, she saw a flash of desire in his eyes, and he stifled a soft groan.

A weird feeling of power rippled through her, and she shivered against him. "Don't move yet, okay?"

He nodded and squeezed his eyes shut as she lifted her head and kissed his neck. She ran her tongue over his neck, tasting and licking, and let her hands drift around his waist and onto his back. She ran her fingers lightly over his back. The muscles contracted under her fingers, and she watched in fascination as a muscle in his jaw ticked violently.

He was still propped above her, his arms holding his weight off of her. She angled her head so she could place a soft, wet kiss on his chest. He groaned, and when she ran her tongue over his flat nipple, he made a short cry and jerked wildly against her.

"Shit. Sorry."

"It's fine." She smiled reassuringly at him before licking and biting his chest.

"Oh my God. Amelia – please," he groaned, his body shuddering.

"I'm good," she said.

"Are you sure?" He asked.

"Yes." She kissed him and moved her hips against his, making him groan into her mouth.

He withdrew and then pushed slowly back into her. He moved his hand down to her thigh and grasped it gently, shifting her leg up so he could sink fully into her.

Amelia moaned encouragingly. The pain had disappeared, leaving a warm, throbbing ache in its place, and her body had stretched around Jack's cock in a way that both surprised and delighted her. The feel of him sliding in and out caused all sorts of delicious feelings deep in her pelvis.

"That feels so good, Jack," she moaned as he thrust in a smooth and easy rhythm.

"I like making you feel good," he said. "Fuck, you're so tight, honey. I'm not going to last long."

With a soft groan, he reached between them. He rubbed her clit as he pumped in and out of her.

His touch on her clit sent fresh desire washing over her,

and she met each of his strokes until, with a soft cry, she came again, her inner muscles squeezing him tight.

Jack growled deep in his throat as his eyes glowed green. His head fell back, a half-moan, half-howl erupting from his throat as he plunged roughly in and out. There was a sudden flood of warmth inside of her, and Jack shook violently before collapsing on top of her warm body. He breathed harshly against her throat, nuzzling her soft skin before he eased out of her and relaxed on his side next to her. He turned her over and spooned her, pulling her back against his chest and cupping her breast before kissing the side of her neck.

"Are you all right, Amelia?" he asked.

"Yes," she said. "I came twice. It was great."

He laughed and dropped another warm kiss on her shoulder.

"Stay in the bed with me?" she asked.

"Yes," he said, resting his head on the pillow behind hers.

CHAPTER 15

Amelia stretched in bed, frowning in confusion at the dull ache in her thighs before remembering what she had done with Jack last night. She glanced behind her. The bed was empty, and she sat straight up, only relaxing when she heard the water running in the bathroom.

With a soft sigh of relief, she collapsed on the bed. She glanced at the alarm clock. It was just after six, and, for the time in years, there had been no dreams of Richard haunting her sleep last night. She stared at the ceiling, and a small smile crossed her lips. Last night had been wonderful.

"No, not wonderful," she whispered out loud. "It was amazing, unbelievable, the best night of my -"

At the sound of her voice, Lupe made a soft 'woof' and leaped onto the bed.

"Lupe, down!" She giggled as he licked at her arms and face. She pushed him to the empty side of the bed, and he laid down next to her, resting his large head on her abdomen. She ran her fingers through the thick scruff of his fur, feeling that lovely blue warmth radiating from him, and scratched behind his ears.

"You is such a good baby," she said in an annoyingly high voice. "Amelia loves her Lupe. Yes, she does. Who's the biggest, fuzziest lapdog in the whole wide world? Is it you?"

"Until he met you, no one would have described him as a lapdog," Jack said dryly from the bathroom doorway.

She smiled at him, her fingers tightening in Lupe's soft fur. "Good morning."

He approached the bed, clicking his fingers at Lupe, who jumped down obediently. He sat down on the bed beside her and rested his hand on her abdomen. "How do you feel?"

"Good." She smiled at him.

"Sore?"

She shrugged. "A little bit. Not bad, though."

He frowned and pulled back the bed covers. Before Amelia could even try to hide her nakedness, he scooped her up and carried her to the bathroom.

"Jack, what are you doing?"

"I ran you a bath," he said.

"Thank you." She smiled at him as he bent over the steaming tub and carefully eased her into the water.

She hissed a little as the hot water flowed between her legs, and Jack frowned. "Is it too hot?"

She shook her head. "No. It's good."

He nodded and stepped back as she sunk to her chin in hot water. She smiled timidly at him. "Why don't you join me?"

"The tub isn't big enough for both of us."

"I can move over." She smiled again at him. "It'll be cozy."

He shook his head again, his face solemn. "I don't think that's a good idea, Amelia."

Her heart dropped to her stomach. Jack was giving her a strange look and being so cool with her. Was he regretting last night? She had thought he enjoyed last night as much as she did, but now, she wasn't sure.

He probably regrets that he allowed himself to be sucked in by your pathetic begging. He told you repeatedly that he didn't want to have sex with you, but you couldn't stop asking him for it, could you?

"Amelia? Are you okay?" Jack asked.

"Yeah, just fine." She picked up the washcloth and ran the soap over it, lathering the soft cloth.

"Amelia -"

"I said I was fine, Jack," she said with sudden impatience. She scrubbed at her leg with rough strokes. "Can you leave me alone, please?"

He scowled at her. "Not until you tell me what's wrong with you."

"What's wrong with me? You're the one who's acting all weird."

"I'm not acting weird." He folded his arms across his chest.

"Look, it's fine if you regret last night. I get it, okay? But could you leave me alone so I can at least salvage the little bit of dignity I have left?"

He knelt beside the tub and pulled the washcloth out of her hand. He pushed her forward and began to wash her back. "You're being ridiculous, Amelia."

She brought her knees up, covering her naked breasts and resting her arms on them. "Then what's your problem? Was I," she swallowed hard, "was I that terrible?"

"No." He ran the washcloth down the curve of her spine. "Last night was – was very enjoyable."

Enjoyable? Amelia wanted to sink into the hot water and not emerge until Jack left.

"Oh, good. I'm so glad I was *enjoyable*," she said, hating the hurt she could hear in her voice.

"No, that didn't come out right." He dipped the washcloth in the warm water and rinsed her back. He lifted and washed her arm, rubbing her skin with hard, circular motions. "I'm angry with myself because I wasn't going to take your virginity last night. I just wanted to make you feel good, and then I lost control."

She stared up at him. "You don't like losing control, do you?"

He shook his head, swiping the washcloth across her underarm before sliding it down her arm and rubbing her wrist. "No, I don't. Your first time should have been with someone normal. Someone who would make it special for you, who would take you out for dinner and buy you flowers, and -"

"You bought Chinese food for me last night," she pointed out.

He laughed, and she grinned at him. "Last night *was* special, Jack. It was the most wonderful night of my life. Don't you get that?"

"I hurt you," he said.

She rolled her eyes. "For God's sake, Jack. You also gave me two incredible orgasms last night. My body is still tingling from them."

She cupped his face. "It barely hurt. And the way you made me feel last night – I had no idea a person could get that much pleasure from another's touch. I don't care who or what you are. You're gentle and kind, and the way you touch me makes me feel so good."

Her voice dropped to a low whisper. "I love the way you touch me."

He leaned in and kissed her, and she moaned softly, her hand gripping his face.

He pulled away and smiled at her before running the soapy washcloth across her upper chest. "Lie back, Amelia."

Shivering a little, she did as he asked. She rested against

the back of the tub and watched as he rubbed the washcloth across her collarbone and over her shoulder.

He moved the washcloth lower, circling first one breast and then the other, smiling with satisfaction when her nipples hardened. He ran the washcloth over one nipple, and she gasped, her back arching as he rubbed the soft cloth over her other nipple.

"Jack," she moaned.

He washed her flat abdomen using large circular motions before he dipped lower, skimming across her pubic bone as she gripped the side of the tub tightly.

"Oh, please," she said.

He rinsed off her breasts and abdomen, then leaned forward and licked away the drop of water that clung to her right nipple before sucking her nipple into his mouth. Her wet hands gripped the back of his head as he sucked hard before circling it with his tongue.

She moaned encouragingly, but he pulled his head free of her hands and reached for the washcloth again. She moved her lower body restlessly, the water rippling and splashing against the side of the tub as he rubbed the soap across the washcloth before dipping the cloth back into the water. He pulled her legs up and washed both her thighs and calves before letting them drop back into the water.

"I think we're done," he teased gently. "Ready to get out of the tub?"

She scowled at him. "You missed a spot."

"Did I?" he asked innocently. "I'm pretty sure I didn't."

"You did," she said. She grabbed the hand holding the washcloth and guided it under the water.

"Right here," she muttered as she opened her thighs and pushed his hand between them.

"Hmm...I should take care of that." He used the washcloth

to rub gently at her soft skin, frowning when she winced a little.

"I did hurt you."

"It's just a little tender. I don't think that's unusual," she said.

Still frowning, he dropped the washcloth and cupped her sex in his large hand. She sighed and arched against his hand as he rubbed gently back and forth. Before long, she was thrusting her pelvis against him, her back arched, and her eyes closed as he rubbed her clit. Water splashed over the side of the tub and onto the floor, and she opened her eyes with an embarrassed grin.

"Oops."

He smiled and stood, reaching for the bath towel as she stood in the tub. He stared at her wet and naked body, his cock rock hard in his briefs, and she blushed and crossed her arms over her breasts.

"No, don't do that," he said, pulling her arms apart and then wrapping the towel around her body. "You're so beautiful, Amelia."

He lifted her out of the tub and quickly dried her off before carrying her into the bedroom. He stood her next to the bed and kissed her hungrily, his hands roaming over her towel-clad body. She returned his kisses, their tongues darting and tasting before he pulled his mouth free and tugged her head back. He kissed down her neck, licking away the small droplets of water as she moaned and twisted against him.

He pulled the towel from her damp body and cupped her bare ass, squeezing it roughly. She groaned and clung to his arms, her knees shaking as hot desire washed over her. He pushed her gently down on the bed until she was lying on her back, her lower legs dangling over the edge of it. He knelt on the floor between her legs, his chest resting against the side of the bed as she sat up a little.

"Jack? What are you -"

Her question turned into a long moan when he kissed the inside of her thigh, his tongue trailing a path to her knee.

"Lay back, honey," he urged, and she obediently fell back onto the bed.

He used his tongue to trace the long, narrow scar that twisted its way from her left knee almost to her hip bone.

"The car accident?" he said against her hip.

"Yes," she moaned as he frowned at the large dark bruise still visible on her hip. He placed a soft, gentle kiss on the bruise before kissing his way to her navel. He circled it with his tongue and blew gently until goosebumps popped up on her pale skin.

She shivered as he placed a kiss in the soft curls at the apex of her thighs, and she opened her legs wide when he kissed his way to her right leg. He traced his tongue down the skin where her thigh met her pelvis, and she made another soft, pleading moan.

He paused, his warm breath brushing across her warm core. "Are you okay up there, Amelia?"

She could almost hear the grin in his voice, and she groaned in frustration. "I'm just fine."

"Good," he said. She jerked when he touched her with rough fingers, parting her wet and swollen lips and exposing her clit. He licked the swollen pink nub with his warm tongue, and she cried out and nearly slid off the end of the bed.

Grinning, he draped her legs over his shoulders and slid his hands under her ass, cupping it and lifting her slightly off the bed.

"Hang on tight, Amelia," he said, dipping his head.

Amelia moaned, her hips rising from the bed and her

heels digging into Jack's back. She had thought nothing could feel better than Jack's fingers against her, but now as he licked and kissed her pussy, she could feel herself rapidly spiralling out of control.

She was almost embarrassed by her lack of control as Jack licked her clit with wide flat strokes of his warm tongue, but she couldn't stop herself from clutching the sheets in her hands and thrusting her pelvis frantically against his face.

"Oh my God!" Waves of pleasure crashed through her pelvis and belly, and she panted and twisted and shook against him.

He sucked her clit into his mouth, and she made a loud cry and arched up off the bed as her orgasm roared through her. She let go of the sheets, her legs falling apart as he cleaned her with his tongue and then kissed the inside of her thighs. He stood, pushing off his briefs, and then knelt on the bed between her legs, urging her thighs further apart and positioning his cock at her wet opening.

"Amelia, look at me," he said. She opened her eyes, staring dazedly up at him, and he leaned down and kissed her gently as he slid his cock into her wet pussy.

Amelia gasped and lifted her legs, wrapping them around his waist as he moved in her. This time there was no pain, just the warm tingling and the feeling of being filled entirely as he plunged his cock deep into her.

She watched his face as he thrust in and out of her. His eyes were squeezed shut, and he panted harshly as he took her. She moved her hips against him, trying to match his rhythm and smiling a little when he groaned with pleasure. She ran her hands across his chest, rubbing her thumb against one flat nipple and watched in fascination as the beard on his face thickened.

He opened his eyes and stared down at her. Her breath

caught in her throat as she watched his eyes turn from brown to green, and he plunged wildly in and out of her.

"Amelia," he groaned. "Oh my God, you feel so good."

She tightened her thighs around his hips and lifted her head, biting roughly at his neck and shoulder. He stiffened, letting out a hoarse how and came deep inside of her before collapsing against her. She rubbed his back, kissing his shoulder and the side of his neck as he shivered.

He lifted his upper body off of her and looked down at her. "That was *very* enjoyable."

She laughed as he rolled onto his side and brought her with him. "Shut up, Jack."

CHAPTER 16

"Are you ready?" Jack asked.

"Yes." Amelia took a deep breath and slid out of the truck. She studied the farmhouse in front of her. There was a large, rust-covered truck in the driveway, and she gave Jack a small smile when he took her glove-covered hand in his.

They walked toward the house together, Lupe loping behind them. The door opened as they approached it, and a woman with dark hair and blue eyes stepped out onto the front porch. A large German shepherd slipped from the house behind her and trotted down the steps. The dog and Lupe sniffed each other curiously as Jack and Amelia paused at the bottom of the stairs.

"Hello, Amelia. My name is Joanna." She smiled at them, but Amelia could see the nerves in it.

"Hello. This is Jack and his dog Lupe."

Joanna nodded to Jack and held the screen door open. "Come inside."

They followed her into the house. It was warm and

smelled vaguely of cinnamon. Amelia glanced around as they followed Joanna into the kitchen.

"Please, sit down." She indicated to the chairs surrounding the large wooden table, and Amelia and Jack sat down. Jack put his arm along the back of her chair and rested his big hand on her neck. He rubbed gently, providing comfort and support with just his touch.

"You're not surprised to see me," Amelia said as Joanna filled a green kettle with water and set it on the stove to boil.

"Your mom called me early this morning. She was worried about you and wanted to know how our meeting went yesterday."

She sat down across from them, and Amelia studied her carefully. They were obviously related. Amelia could see the resemblance in the curve of her cheekbones and the shape of her eyes.

"I imagine this was quite a shock to you," Joanna said.

Amelia barked harsh laughter. "You could say that."

"I'm sorry, Amelia. But you should know that your mom and dad always intended to tell you and your brother. They had already spoken to us about it before the accident."

"Yeah, I heard." Amelia glanced around the kitchen. "Is your husband home?"

"Bill died two years ago."

"I'm sorry," Amelia said.

"Thank you. He was a good man, my Bill. I was grocery shopping, and he was here working in the garden. He had a heart attack."

"I'm so sorry," Amelia said again. Despite her anger and confusion, she could feel a thread of sorrow for the woman. The pain on her face was evident, and Amelia couldn't imagine how difficult it must have been.

"If I had been home, I could have saved him," Joanna said with a hitch in her voice. "But I wasn't, and I didn't."

Amelia frowned. "I don't understand."

Joanna stared at the gloves on her hands. "Do you always wear gloves, Amelia?"

"Yes. I don't like people touching me."

Joanna looked at Jack. "But he can touch you?"

"He's different." Amelia looked down as Lupe rested his head on her lap and whined softly. She petted his head as Joanna's dog also shoved her head onto her lap.

Joanna smiled a little. "Luna seems to have taken a liking to you and your wolf."

"He's a hybrid," Jack said.

"Is he?" She raised one eyebrow at him and then stood to pour them all cups of tea. She placed the cups in front of them, and Amelia took a cautious sip of the hot liquid.

Joanna blew out her breath. "Your father – your biological father - had the same gift as you."

Amelia stiffened in her chair as Jack leaned forward and pushed away his cup of tea before giving Joanna a guarded look. "What do you mean?"

She smiled at him. "When people touched him, he could hear their thoughts, feel their emotions, and absorb their memories."

Amelia stared in shock at her. She didn't notice when Lupe whined softly and licked at her arm. "He was like me?"

"Yes," Joanna said. "I was immune to him as Jack is to you, but everyone else was an open book. Including you and your brother."

Amelia sat back in her chair, her face white and her hands trembling. Jack put his arm around her and squeezed her shoulder lightly. "Amelia, are you okay?"

She nodded as Joanna said, "You need to know something, Amelia. Your dad and I – we loved you and Richard so much. We were so happy when you were born and wanted to give you everything. We had hoped and prayed during the pregnancy that you would be immune to your father like I was. It was so horrible for your dad when you weren't."

Amelia swallowed hard. "So, that's why you gave us up? Because our father couldn't touch us?"

Joanna nodded. "Yes."

"Jesus," Amelia said. "Couldn't he have worn gloves or something? Couldn't you have figured out a way to – to…"

"To what, my love?" Joanna asked softly.

When Amelia didn't reply, Joanna said, "You know how difficult this gift is. You know what it's like to be afraid to touch people, never knowing if they'll brush up against you accidentally and you'll be privy to their most intimate secrets. Your father would never have been able to hold you, hug you, and kiss your sweet faces. Would you have wanted to live with a father who would always have to keep a distance between you?"

Amelia thought about her father when she was a child. She had very clear memories of him chasing her around the house, tickling her and blowing raspberries on her belly as she had giggled and shrieked and kicked her feet at him. She could remember him carrying her to bed, holding her tight against his broad chest, and dropping soft kisses on her face as he tucked her into bed.

Joanna watched her face, a bitter smile on her lips. "You see, my love? It would have been so terribly awful for you, Richard, and your father."

Luna nudged her nose under Joanna's hand, and she rubbed the dog's ears absently. "I hope you can understand how difficult it was for us to give you both up. We knew that Laura and Walter would love you and give you what we couldn't, but it still nearly destroyed us. Laura was very kind to us and sent letters and pictures through the years."

Tears were beginning to spill down her cheeks, and she

wiped at them angrily. "When Richard died, we almost told you, but Laura and Walter said that you were having a difficult time with Richard's death and that you had become withdrawn and depressed. We didn't want to make it worse."

Amelia reached for Jack's hand. "When I woke up in the hospital, I could suddenly hear and feel people's thoughts when they touched me. My mom hugged me, and…it doesn't matter now. I was hit in the head and was in a coma. I thought it had something to do with that."

"It was the onset of puberty. Our gifts don't develop until after puberty. You would have started hearing people's thoughts even if you hadn't had the accident. Did Richard show any signs of a gift?" Joanna asked.

"No. Both of us were perfectly normal. And it's not a gift – it's a curse. I'm thankful that Richard didn't have to live with this."

Joanna sighed. "We don't all have the same gifts. Just because you and your father had the same one, it does not mean that Richard would have had it as well. He could have been blessed with another."

Jack frowned. "What other gifts?"

"There are things in this world that cannot be explained. There are," Joanna paused and stared appraisingly at Jack, "creatures who walk the earth as humans but aren't."

"You mean like vampires?" Amelia said.

Joanna nodded, "There are many different types of paranormals – vampires, faeries, seers, and Lycan – the list goes on."

Amelia gripped Jack's hand hard, glancing up at him. He gave her a reassuring smile, and she turned back to Joanna.

"So, you're saying I'm not human or a paranormal?"

Joanna shrugged. "In a way, yes. I prefer to think of us as humans who have evolved."

"How many are there of us?"

"Many. We are scattered worldwide, and we have many different gifts."

"You keep saying that – what other gifts?" Jack asked.

"Some of us can control the elements of the earth, some can predict the future, and I know of a woman only two towns over who can speak with the animals. Some can sense when danger is coming to them, and some can heal with only a touch. There are probably more gifts that I am unaware of."

Amelia sat quietly, trying to absorb everything she'd just heard. She was oddly comforted to know that there were others like her. It made her feel less like a freak.

She studied Joanna before asking, "What's your gift?"

"Let me show you." Joanna stood. "You're hurt, yes? Your hip?"

"How do you know that?" Amelia asked.

"Will you stand and show it to me?" Joanna asked.

Amelia stood and lifted her shirt, pushing her jean skirt down to reveal the dark bruise on her hip.

"It looks very sore," Joanna said.

Jack stood and moved behind Amelia. When Joanna reached toward the bruise, he pushed her hand away and wrapped his arm around Amelia's waist. "Don't touch her."

"Jack, it's fine." Amelia stroked his arm. "Let her show me."

"And if you're not immune to her?" Jack asked.

"There's only one way to find out," Amelia said.

"What are you going to do to her?" He stared at Joanna, who gave him a small smile.

"I won't hurt her, Lycan. I promise you that."

"How did you know he's a Lycan?" Amelia asked.

"Call it an educated guess," Joanna said. "Are you ready?"

Amelia nodded and steeled herself as Joanna placed her

soft hand against the bruise. She closed her eyes as Joanna's thoughts and feelings immediately crowded into her brain.

Tears slipped down her cheeks, and vaguely, she was aware of Jack growling deep in his throat. "Get your hands off of her."

She opened her eyes as Jack pulled her away from Joanna. She stared at her biological mother. Joanna's face was pale, and her lips were trembling, but she smiled at Amelia. "I'm sorry, my love. I wish I were immune to you."

Jack turned her toward him and cupped her face. "Are you okay, honey?" He wiped at the tears on her face with one rough thumb.

"I'm fine." She kissed the line of his jaw, breathing deeply before turning back to face Joanna. "I'm sorry. Are you okay?"

Joanna nodded. "Yes. I'm sad that I'm not immune to you."

"I – it wasn't so bad touching you," Amelia admitted. "I could feel how much you...."

"Love you?" Joanna said.

Amelia nodded. "Yes. I still don't understand what your gift is, though."

Joanna pointed silently to her side, and Amelia glanced down, her eyes widening. The bruise on her hip was gone entirely, and she ran a disbelieving hand over her side, pressing firmly into the skin and shaking her head when there was no pain.

"You're a healer," Jack said.

"I am. I can sense when people are hurt and heal them with my touch," Joanna said.

"So that's what you meant when you said you could have saved him if you had been home," Amelia said.

"Yes. There isn't a single moment where I don't regret leaving your father that day." Joanna wiped at the tears that were running down her face. "He would have been so excited to meet you, sweet Amelia."

"I would have liked to have met him too," Amelia said.

After a moment, Joanna cleared her throat. "Will you sit down again? I'll tell you everything I know about our people."

CHAPTER 17

"How are you doing?" Jack gave Amelia a worried look as he parked in front of her house.

She shrugged. "Okay, I think. It's a lot to take in."

She slid out of the truck, Lupe jumping down behind her, and met Jack at the front. He rubbed her arms, and she leaned against him. She rested her head on his chest and listened to the solid beat of his heart.

"At least I know I'm not the only one out there," she said.

He brushed her hair back from her face and kissed her forehead. "That's good news. You may even find someone of your own kind who is immune to you. Your father did."

His stomach churned with nausea at the thought of her with someone other than him.

She stiffened against him. "Maybe," she muttered before pulling away.

Jack reached for her hand, folding her small hand into his large one. "Amelia, I'm not trying to upset you. It's just – you know that we can't have a long-term relationship. Humans and Lycans are not meant to mate for life."

"Your parents did," she said.

"And look what happened to them," he said harshly.

"Your adoptive parents have done just fine. They -"

"They were cut off from their pack and forced to live alone and raise their children as outcasts." He could hear the anger in his voice. "Trust me, Amelia. Being my mate would only make your situation worse. You would be an outcast with your people and an outcast with mine. I have to live that life, but I'll be damned if I ever force someone else into it."

"Maybe you should let me make my own decisions." She was starting to get angry and yanked her hand out of his. "In case you haven't noticed, I'm already an outcast."

"I won't make it worse by making you my mate," he said.

"You said it was more acceptable now," she reminded him. "You said that more and more Lycans are accepting humans into their packs. Besides, how can I be rejected by your pack when you don't even have one?"

He winced, hurt crossing his face, and a look of shame covered hers. "I'm sorry, Jack. That was a terrible thing to say, and I am deeply sorry."

"It's fine, Amelia. You're right. I don't have a pack."

She rested her hand on his arm. "I shouldn't have said that. You do have a pack. You have your parents, and you have Hank."

He nodded but didn't say anything. Amelia wasn't a Lycan. She could never understand the sorrow and loss a Lycan felt without a pack. Hell, he hardly understood it himself. It was a little easier for him – he had grown up without a pack. Despite Joy's happiness with her family and how much she loved Tom, he and Hank could sense how she yearned for her pack. He and Hank felt that same yearning despite their different upbringing from most Lycans. They couldn't help it. It was in their nature to be in a pack, and there would always be a sense of loss if they weren't. Joy hid it well from Tom. As far as Jack could tell, his adoptive father never suspected she even craved to be with a pack again. But based on the warm look of sympathy Amelia was giving him, he suspected that she already sensed his desire to be a part of a pack.

"Jack?" Amelia rubbed his arm. "Are you okay?"

"I'm fine," he said. "You're freezing. Let's get in the house."

He took her hand and led her towards the house. As they approached the porch steps, Lupe growled softly, and Jack pulled Amelia close.

"Amelia, wait," he said. He lifted his head and inhaled deeply.

"Jack? What is it?"

"They were here."

She slipped closer to him, wrapping her arm around his waist and taking comfort in his solid warmth. "Are they still here?"

She looked around nervously. It was late morning, and the sun shone brightly, but she felt exposed and vulnerable.

"I don't think so. C'mon."

They walked up the steps, and Jack reached for the door. Amelia made a small moan of dismay at the damage to the door around the lock and handle.

"Go and get in the truck, please, Amelia." Jack pushed her gently toward the steps.

"No, I'm staying with you," she said.

"No, you're not. Get into my truck, and if anyone who isn't me comes out of the door, you drive away."

"Like hell, I will," she said.

He pressed the keys to his truck into her shaking hand. "Go, Amelia," he said.

"No." She folded her arms across her chest, and he growled at her stubbornness.

"Stop growling at me," she said.

"Do what I say," he said.

151

She shook her head stubbornly. "I won't leave you."

He gave her a little shake. "I'll find you. Drive to the sheriff's office, and I'll meet you there."

"I don't like this, Jack," she said.

He kissed her roughly, his hands cupping her face and his mouth warm on hers.

"It'll be fine, Amelia. I'll be back out in a minute."

He pulled away from her and waited until she and Lupe had climbed into the truck before he disappeared into the house. Amelia sat in the driver's seat, holding Jack's keys and darting nervous glances around her. Lupe sat beside her, a low, continuous growl rumbling from his chest. Five agonizingly slow minutes ticked by, and she was just about to go into the house despite Jack's orders when he reappeared on the porch.

She released her breath in a harsh rush, climbing out of the truck and running across the yard with Lupe at her heels. She nearly fell into Jack's arms. "Are you okay?"

He nodded, but his face was pale, and he was giving her a look she didn't understand.

"What's wrong?" she asked

"Amelia, they were in your house, and ... they ransacked it. They -"

She pushed away from him and ran through the front door. She looked around, her mouth dropping open with dismay. Her formerly tidy home looked like a hurricane had gone through it. Her couch and rocking chair had been torn apart in the living room. The pictures on the wall were smashed on the floor, and deep furrows were dug into the walls. She shivered, easily picturing the claws that had made those marks.

She walked into the kitchen. Every item in her cupboards had been pulled out and dropped on the floor. Broken dishes and glass littered the entire kitchen. Food from her pantry and fridge was smeared on the walls, and the front of the fridge had a massive dent in it.

"Oh my God," she said as Jack joined her. "Why did they do this?"

"I don't know," he said. "I've never seen Lycans do anything like this before."

"Are you sure it was Lycans?" she asked.

He nodded. "I can smell them."

Amelia suddenly stiffened and then raced for her bedroom.

"Amelia! Wait!" He reached for her, fingers skating across her sleeve, but she slipped past him and sprinted down the hallway.

"Please God, please God, please God," she chanted. Like the other rooms, her bedroom had been wrecked, and she stumbled over a large pile of her clothing as she struggled to get to the nightstand that was lying on its side. The contents of its drawers were strewn around it, and she pawed through them frantically, looking for the small blue box.

She breathed a sigh of relief when she found it partially hidden under a t-shirt. She lifted it, her hands trembling, and took a deep breath when she opened it and found the silver chain and cross still nestled against the blue fabric.

"Amelia?" Jack knelt beside her, and she gave him a look of relief.

"This was Richard's. It's the only thing I have left of him now. I was afraid that…."

Her voice died in her throat as she glanced over Jack's shoulder. Her eyes widened, and she could almost feel the blood draining from her face.

"Don't look at that, honey," Jack said.

"Jack, is that - is that blood?"

He nodded grimly. "I think so."

He helped her to her feet and tried to turn her face away. She shook him free. "Is it human blood?"

"I don't know, honey."

Amelia swallowed, feeling ill to her stomach and a little faint. The message on the wall was only three words, but it sent adrenaline through her body and made her feel like there wasn't enough oxygen in the room.

Amelia, be mine.

The words covered most of the wall and had dried to a dark red that looked almost black.

"What's going on, Jack?" she asked. "I don't – I mean, why are they doing this? They don't even know me."

"I don't know, but I'm about to find out."

He led her from the bedroom, and she followed him back to the porch. He sat her on one of the wicker chairs and took her cold hands in his.

"You wait here while I get you some clothes and some toiletries. It's not safe to stay in the house."

"I won't be chased from my own home, Jack."

He cupped her face. "It'll just be for tonight. I promise you."

He disappeared into the house before she could ask him what he meant. She sat numbly on the porch with Lupe leaning against her leg. When her neighbour Amy walked by with her dog Terrence and waved cheerfully at her, she waved back. It was cold. She could see her breath pluming out in front of her, but the sun shone brightly, and the sky was a brilliant blue. She could hardly believe that her house was in shambles and that a group of Lycans had left her a message written in blood.

Jack returned in less than fifteen minutes. He held her small suitcase and closed the door carefully behind her. "C'mon, Amelia. We need to go."

"Where are we going?" she asked, following him and Lupe

to his truck. He lifted her into the truck, Lupe leaping in gracefully behind her, and slid behind the wheel.

"I'm taking you to Ray's office. We'll let him know that your house was broken into and someone left you a threatening message. You can stay with him at the sheriff's office until I return."

"Get back?" She looked at him in bewilderment. "Where are you going?"

"I'm going to find the Lycans who did this," he said grimly. He started his truck, but before he could put it into gear, she crowded up against him, gripping his arm tightly.

"No! You are not going after them alone, Jack." Panic was sinking into her, making her lungs seize up.

"I have to, honey. If I take Ray with me or any other humans, there's the possibility that they could get seriously hurt."

"You could get seriously hurt!"

Lycans live by specific rules. They won't hurt me. They would never harm another of their kind for no reason. I'm only going to speak with the pack leader, find out why they want you and ask them to leave you alone."

"I don't like this," she said as he drove toward the sheriff's office.

"I swear to you that it'll be fine. I'll be back before you know it."

"But Jack, these Lycans don't seem like they're normal Lycans. You said you had no idea why they would do this to my house," she said.

He smiled reassuringly. "They're still not going to hurt one of their kind. Trust me, okay?"

She pulled her cell phone out of her pocket. "Give me your cell phone, Jack."

He handed it to her without question, and she quickly added her name and number to his contacts before adding his to hers. She hesitated and then scrolled through his contacts until she found Hank's number. She entered it into her phone and then handed his phone back to him.

"Let me come with you," she said.

"No. It's you they want. I'm not letting you get anywhere near them," he said.

She glanced down at her phone, inspiration striking her when she saw Hank's name in her contacts. "Call Hank. Ask him to go with you."

"It'll take Hank two hours to get here. We don't have that kind of time. I can follow their scent, but it'll have faded by the time Hank gets here."

They were nearing the sheriff's office, and her desperation kicked it up a notch. "Please call him, Jack. I know you'll go anyway, but I'd feel better if he was here. If something goes wrong, Hank's the only one who will know what to do."

He pulled into the parking lot and stared at her for a moment. "All right, honey."

She sighed with relief and hugged Lupe as Jack called Hank's number.

CHAPTER 18

Amelia paced back and forth in the lobby of the sheriff's office. Susan gave her a sympathetic look, but Amelia couldn't muster up the energy to say anything.

Jack had given Ray an abbreviated version of what happened at her home. He hadn't shared any information about the Lycans and told Ray that he needed to return to the city for a few hours and return before nightfall for Amelia.

She had begged him to take Lupe with her, but he refused. "He'll keep you safe until I get back, honey," he said before kissing her. "I'll return soon. I promise."

She'd had to force herself not to cling to him like a crybaby when he left.

Ray had sent two deputies to her house to photograph the damage, and he'd taken Amelia's statement himself. It had been brief. Unable to share the truth with him, Amelia could only shake her head and murmur that she didn't know why anyone would be after her.

"Amelia? Sit down, honey. You'll wear a hole in the floor," Susan said.

Amelia shook her head and continued to pace. Lupe

followed her closely, whining now and then until she petted and soothed him. The wolf was as nervous and tense as she was. His ears stood straight up, and the hair on the back of his neck kept rising. His tail was tucked between his legs, and whenever someone got too close to Amelia, he would growl softly.

Amelia's stomach was in knots, and her hands were sweating inside her gloves. She didn't care what Jack said. It didn't feel right to her that he had gone after the Lycans himself, and she cursed herself for the hundredth time for letting him leave.

The bell over the front door jingled, and she could have sobbed with relief when Hank's large frame filled the doorway.

"Hank!" She ran toward Jack's brother. She took his hand and squeezed it tight.

Lupe weaved anxiously around his feet, and Hank reached down and scratched the wolf's head.

"Is he back yet?" he asked in a low voice.

She shook her head. "No. I can't believe you're here already."

"Sometimes, being a cop has its advantages. I sped most of the way here."

"We need to talk, Hank," Amelia said. "Something isn't right about this. I know it isn't."

He nodded and glanced up as Ray came out of his office. "Can I help you?"

"Ray, this is Jack's brother, Hank. He's a detective as well."

Ray shook his hand. "You were in the other day, right?"

"Yes, sir." Hank glanced down at Amelia as Ray frowned.

"Your brother went back to the city. Did you not know that?"

"I do. He should be back shortly. He sent me out to keep an eye on Amelia."

Ray bristled a little. "We can take care of our own here, Detective Emerson."

"He knows that, Ray," Amelia said. "Jack is just being cautious."

Ray continued to frown as Hank held his hand out to Amelia. "Let's go get some lunch, Amelia."

She took his hand as Ray crossed his arms over his chest. "I think you should stay here, Amelia. We have no idea who's after you. For all we know, they could be watching you."

"I'll be fine. Hank won't let anything happen to me, and besides, I'm starving. I'll pass out if I don't get something to eat soon."

She tried to smile naturally at Ray before following Hank outside.

* * *

JACK MOVED DEEPER INTO THE WOODS. HE HAD BEEN following the trail on foot for nearly three hours, and he didn't like how quiet the woods were. He had followed the scent from Amelia's house into the forest, and he wasn't surprised when he found himself close to the cabin where Ed had taken his wife and baby girl. He walked quietly, listening intently for the sounds of his kind, and inhaled deeply every few minutes.

He was nervous. He had told Amelia that Lycans didn't hurt their kind without reason. He wasn't lying, but she had picked up too quickly on the fact that these Lycans were abnormal. The truth was that he had no idea what to expect from the pack. All he knew was that he needed to find out what they wanted from Amelia and convince them to leave her alone.

He squinted through the trees. There was a circular clearing just up ahead, and as he entered it, the smell of his kind deepened. He stopped in the clearing and waited, knowing they were in the trees and watching him.

When no one came forward, he said, "I wish to speak to your pack leader."

There was more silence, and he frowned. "You would deny me this courtesy?"

There was a rustling, and a man stepped out. He wore jeans, his chest and feet were bare, and a long twisting scar ran across his chest.

Jack nodded to him. "Are you the pack leader?"

"No. Why are you here?"

"I have a matter to discuss with your leader." As Jack spoke, there was more movement, and about fifteen men and women silently emerged from the trees. A woman, short in stature with brown skin and dark hair to her waist, stood next to the man with the scar. She took his hand and stared at Jack solemnly. Jack's heart thudded heavily in his chest, but he allowed no emotion to show on his face.

He caught a familiar scent, and a growl erupted from his throat. The redhead from Amelia's room had stepped out of the trees. He stood next to the scarred man and his mate, and Jack bared his teeth and snarled at him.

The redhead stepped back, a brief look of fear crossing his face as he rested his hand on his side. Jack grinned fiercely at him as the man with the scar squeezed the redhead's arm reassuringly.

"Relax, Eric. He's not here to harm you."

He glanced up at Jack. "You did a lot of damage to my brother, Lycan."

"He shouldn't have tried to take what is mine," Jack snapped.

The man frowned. "She is your mate?"

Before Jack could reply, a man stepped into the clearing. He was big. He stood nearly half a foot taller than Jack's 6'4" and outweighed him by at least seventy pounds. His skin was brown from the sun, and a layer of hair covered his body. His beard was thick and bushy, and a trickle of fear ran down Jack's back when his gaze landed on him.

The Lycan had gone mad. Jack could see it in his muddy brown eyes, could smell it on his scent, and he glanced warily at the man with the scar. The man stared back impassively, but Jack knew he could sense his leader's madness.

"She is not his mate, Anthony." The man laughed. "Perhaps she has mated with him, but he has not claimed her for his own."

He winked at Jack. "Am I not right, half-breed?"

"The woman belongs to me. What interest do you have in her?" Jack said.

"I wish to have her as my mate."

"That will never happen," Jack growled.

The pack leader laughed. "Do not be so sure of that, half-breed."

"What interest do you have in a human?" Jack asked. He glanced around the circle of men and women. "There are no half-breeds here. I don't think that's an accident."

The man shrugged. "You and I both know that full-blood Lycans are becoming increasingly rare. Perhaps I have decided to give in to the inevitable and breed with the humans."

"Bullshit," Jack said.

The man laughed again. "I like you. If you weren't a half-breed who reeked of humans, I'd ask you to join our pack."

He hesitated. "Of course, I am about to have my own half-breeds running around."

"Amelia is mine," Jack repeated.

The man's face grew dark, and he knotted his big hands into fists. "You cannot keep her to yourself. Not when she has such marvelous power."

"She has no powers," Jack said.

"Do not lie to me!" The man suddenly roared. Several of his pack members whimpered and stepped back, staring at the ground at their feet.

"We caught the vampire on our lands, and before I killed him, he told me everything he knew about your Amelia. I felt her power running through his veins!" The pack leader's face was turning red, and the hair on his body was thickening as he began to shift.

"David, calm down." Anthony stepped toward the larger man. David swung his meaty arm out and slammed it against Anthony's face with a low howl. He fell back, landing on the ground with a hard thud as the woman standing with Anthony made a loud cry of distress and knelt next to him.

She stared up at David with something close to hatred in her eyes as she and Eric helped Anthony to his feet. She cupped his face, staring at the dripping cut over Anthony's eye.

"I'm fine, Leah." Anthony tugged his head free from her hands and tucked her behind him.

"Do not interrupt me when I am speaking to our guest, Anthony," David said.

Anthony gave him a strained smile. "Forgive me, David. It won't happen again."

"I will take Amelia as my mate, half-breed," David said to Jack. "She will give me children who will have my strength and speed and her abilities. My children will be powerful Lycans. All other Lycans will bow before them."

"I will kill you before I let you take her from me. Do you understand?" Jack said.

"You believe you can beat me, half-breed?" David grinned.

"I do." Jack stared steadily at David, pleased when a brief flicker of uncertainty crossed the Lycan's face.

David straightened his shoulders. "That will never happen, half-breed." He turned to the pack. "Kill him."

Anthony's mate let out a soft gasp, and Anthony stared at David in shock. "David, this is not our way. The woman is his mate. If you want her for yourself, then you must challenge him."

"Once more, Anthony," David said softly. "Defy me just once more, and your pretty little mate will see your head on a pole."

He turned back to the rest of the pack. "Kill him and bring his body back to me."

When they hesitated, he glared at them furiously. "I am your alpha! You will do as I say! Do you understand that?"

They nodded grimly, and he smiled at Jack. "Goodbye, half-breed. Make sure you are in your wolf form when my people kill you. I want to skin you of your pelt and use it as a rug in my home. Perhaps it will be my wedding gift to Amelia."

Jack's cool broke with his words, and with a loud howl, he lunged for David. In an instant, the pack of humans had transformed into their Lycan forms, and they drove him back with snarling and snapping of their teeth.

David laughed and shifted. He turned and loped away as his pack closed in around Jack. Only Anthony, his mate, and the redheaded Lycan remained human as David disappeared into the forest.

"Brothers and sisters do not do this. David has gone mad. Can you not feel it?" Anthony said. "This is not our way, and you know that."

The pack ignored him, circling closer and closer to Jack.

As a large black wolf on his left crouched, Jack took a deep breath and shifted to his Lycan form. The black wolf leaped for him, and Jack met him in mid-air. Howling and snarling, the two wolves tangled together, falling to the ground and rolling in the dirt as they snapped and bit at each other viciously.

There was a strangled cry and a loud snap as Jack pinned the other wolf to the ground and snapped his neck with one twist of his head. The other wolves howled in shock and sorrow and leaped on Jack as he turned to face them.

Growling and snapping, Jack disappeared under the writhing, howling pack of wolves.

CHAPTER 19

"Have you ever heard of Lycans doing that before, Hank?" Amelia stared out the car window.

After leaving the sheriff's office, they grabbed a quick bite to eat, and Amelia gave Hank more details of what had happened.

"No, I haven't," he said.

She glanced at him. "Where are we going?"

"Back to your place. I want to see if there's any scent left that I can follow."

"I'm so worried about him, Hank. I should never have let him go out there alone."

"Good luck trying to stop him. He's the most stubborn guy I know," Hank said.

He pulled up in front of her house. Jack's truck was parked there, and Amelia's heart leaped in her chest.

"Maybe he's back?" she said hopefully.

"I doubt it," Hank said. "He most likely followed the scent on foot."

The two of them exited the car, and Amelia watched with interest as Hank and Lupe went around to the back of the house and began sniffing. When Hank dropped to his knees and carefully sniffed the ground, she glanced nervously at her neighbour's window. She hoped they wouldn't choose this moment to look outside.

"Anything?" she asked.

"No. There's a scent, but it's way too faint. And it'll only get fainter the further we move away from the house."

He sighed and stared at Lupe. The wolf whined and nudged his head against Hank's hand. Hank scratched his ears as he stared quietly at the wolf.

"Do you have any ideas of how else to track him?" Amelia asked.

He didn't reply at first, and she was about to repeat herself when he said, "Amelia, I need you to think carefully. Are there people in this town who keep themselves cut off from everyone else?"

She frowned. "I wouldn't know. I'm one of those people."

He paced back and forth in the yard. "They would be a smaller group, more men than women, and they wouldn't live in town. They might work in town and do their grocery shopping here, but they wouldn't have much contact with the people in the town. They would live either right in the woods or on the outskirts of it."

She rubbed at her forehead for a few minutes, staring down at the ground before looking up at him hesitantly. "There was a group a few years ago that Ray had some trouble with. Some teens camping in the woods said the group had a dog that tried to bite them. Ray smoothed it over with the teen's parents. He said the group out in the woods had lived there for years. I think a few of them work for Jim Traden's construction company, but I'm not positive."

She stuck her hands in the pockets of her jacket. "Do you think they're the Lycan pack?"

Hank shrugged. "It's a good enough place to start as any. Do you know where they are?"

"They're out by Miller's Crossing. About four or five miles into the woods, there's a road that…."

She looked at him, her eyes widening. "Hank, the night that Jack saved me from the vampire, we were close to Miller's Crossing. Jack howled, and there were – were answering howls."

She slapped herself in the head. "Oh my God. I'm so stupid. Why didn't I think of that before?"

Hank took her gloved hand and led her back to the car. "Come on. Let's get out to this Miller's Crossing."

"I don't know exactly where they live. I know the back roads to Miller's Crossing, but that's it," she said as Hank reached under the front fender of Jack's truck and pulled out a small black box. He opened it and popped the spare key out.

"It doesn't matter. If we're close enough, I'll be able to smell them. We'll take Jack's truck. It's better suited to country roads than my damn car is." He opened the truck's door, and Lupe jumped in before Amelia climbed up.

Amelia clicked her seatbelt in place as Hank started the truck. "How long has Jack been gone?"

She glanced at her watch. "Almost three hours, I think."

He smiled reassuringly at her. "We'll find him. Don't worry, okay?"

She gave him a wavering smile in return. "Okay."

* * *

ANTHONY STARED AT LEAH AND HIS BROTHER. "THIS ISN'T right. I won't watch our pack kill an innocent Lycan. We must help him."

"We'll be turned out from the pack, Anthony," Eric said.

His eyes were huge, and he flinched when Jack made a howl of pain.

Anthony turned to Leah and took her cold hands in his own. "I have to help him. You know I do."

"I know," she said.

He shifted and turned, barking and snarling loudly as he approached the group of wolves tearing into Jack.

Eric looked at Leah. Her eyes were glowing, and with a sudden short howl, she shifted and joined her mate.

"Aww, shit!" Eric scowled and shifted, bounding forward to help his brother and Leah.

* * *

"Hank?" Amelia panted as she hurried to catch up with him. "Are we close?"

"I think so." He was inhaling deeply, and he gave her an apologetic look. "I need to shift. It's easier to track in my Lycan form."

"Okay."

He stripped off his jacket and shirt, and she turned around, giving him some privacy. Lupe leaned against her, his ears up and his entire body alert as he scanned the woods around them. They were about two miles from the cabin, and she clasped her arms around her body and shivered lightly.

There was a sharp bark behind her, and she turned to see Hank in his Lycan form. He was as big as Jack, but his fur was a much darker grey. He barked again as Lupe whined eagerly and stared up at Amelia.

She nodded, but there was a loud howling from deep in the woods before they could continue. Although she wasn't positive that it was Jack, the hair on the back of Amelia's neck stood up. She glanced at Hank. He stood perfectly still, and his thick fur pelt was completely on end. He seemed almost frozen as another loud howl of pain split the air. Standing next to her, Lupe voiced a howl of despair in response. Amelia clapped her hands to her ears, wincing as Lupe sent up another wailing cry into the cold air.

The sound seemed to break Hank of his spell, and, with another short bark, he tore off into the woods. Lupe bounded after him, and Amelia, her heart pounding and the metallic taste of fear in her mouth, chased after them.

She lost them quickly in the trees, but she easily followed the sound of snarls and howls. She ran and ran, the noises steadily growing louder. There were short yips of pain drowned out by loud growling and howls, and she took a deep breath and forced herself to run faster. A stitch formed in her side, and she placed her hand against the throbbing pain as she scrambled over a fallen log. A low-hanging branch swiped across her face, cutting her cheek deeply. She ignored the blood dripping down her smooth flesh.

She ran past a large oak tree and tripped over an exposed root, nearly falling into the clearing. Her breath caught in her throat. There were Lycans everywhere. Hank and Lupe, as well as three Lycans she didn't recognize, stood in the middle of the clearing and formed a protective circle around Jack. He was lying on his side, and fear stabbed through her heart. She couldn't tell if he was breathing from where she was.

As she watched, one of the wolves darted forward. Its head was low, and it tried to reach around Hank to bite at Jack's side. Moving so quickly he was a blur, Hank lunged forward, and the wolf screamed in agony as Hank's teeth sank into his neck. The wolf tore itself free from Hank's grip. There was a large gaping bite in its neck, and the blood poured steadily from it as the wolf turned and slunk into the woods with its tail between its legs. After a moment, the other wolves retreated into the forest.

Amelia ran across the clearing, slipping between Lupe and Hank and dropping to her knees beside Jack's still body.

"Please, God, please, God," she begged as she reached for his body with numb fingers. She rested her hand against his side, ignoring the sounds of the wolves around her, and let out a sobbing gasp of relief when she felt the gentle rise of his side.

"Jack? Honey, can you hear me?" She stroked the side of the wolf's head.

He didn't stir, and she called his name again. Hank shifted into his human form and knelt naked next to her.

"Is he alive?" he asked.

"Yes." She stroked Jack's fur again.

She blinked when the three wolves shifted into their human forms. She stared at them numbly for a moment. One was a woman with long hair and brown skin, the other was the redhead who had tried to kidnap her, and the last was the man with the scar. The one she had seen in the redhead's thoughts.

All three of them were naked, panting, and bleeding from various wounds. She tensed as they crowded around them and held out one gloved hand. "Stay away. I'm warning you."

The man with the scar held up his hands. "We're here to help you."

She glanced at Hank, and he nodded. "They were driving the other Lycans away from Jack when I showed up."

Before she could reply, Jack made a low whine and then coughed harshly.

"Jack?" She leaned closer, jerking back when he suddenly shifted to his human form. He opened his eyes and stared blearily at her. They were full of confusion and pain, and she kissed him lightly.

"Amelia?" he rasped.

"Hi, honey," she said. Tears slipped down her cheeks, and

she glanced up as Hank sucked in his breath. She stared at his white, frightened face before following his gaze.

"Oh my God," she moaned as she studied the gaping wound in Jack's side. Blood poured out of it, soaking into the ground, and she ripped off her jacket and pressed it on the wound as hard as she could.

Jack gave a low cry of pain and shifted to his Lycan form.

"We have to help him!" Amelia said. "He needs to go to the hospital!"

She pressed the fabric harder against his fur as Jack turned back to human with another soft pop. He shifted back and forth as they watched helplessly.

"We can't take him to the hospital like this," Hank said. "He's too badly wounded to control the shift. If they see him like this, they'll..." He drove one ham-sized fist into the ground.

"Will he heal on his own?" Amelia asked. "If we bandage him, clean the wound, will he start to heal?"

"I don't know," Hank said. "He has so many injuries. Wounds from other Lycans take longer to heal than normal wounds."

Amelia scanned Jack's body. Hank was right. The wound on his side was the worst, but his entire body was covered in bites and scratches. There was a long, trailing gash down his back, and blood dripped down his leg from a large bite out of his thigh.

The woman knelt beside Jack and placed her hand on his back. "He is a half-breed. His healing ability will not be as strong as a full-blood."

"Goddammit!" Hank shouted. "What the hell do we do?"

Amelia stared at Jack. Her mind raced with fear and confusion, and she closed her eyes and took three deep breaths.

Think, Amelia, think.

Lupe sat beside her, whining continuously, and she forced herself to block out the sound of his crying. After a moment, her eyes popped open, and she stared at the three naked Lycans. "I know who we can take him to. Can you help us carry him?"

They hesitated, and she gave them a pleading look. "Please. He'll die if you don't. You know he will."

"Anthony," the woman said softly, looking up at him.

He nodded grimly. "I know."

He bent down and grabbed Jack's legs. "Eric, help the big one take his front. Leah, support his middle. And for Christ's sake, don't drop him when he shifts."

The four of them lifted Jack carefully and followed Amelia out of the clearing.

* * *

THE RUSTY TRUCK WAS SITTING IN THE DRIVEWAY WHEN HANK turned down the dusty road, and Amelia could have sobbed with relief. She sat in the truck's back seat with Jack's large body draped across her lap and Leah's. She had ripped off her shirt, wrapping it around the bite in his thigh. The thin material was soaked in blood, and she could see blood dripping steadily down his leg. Hank had given her his shirt for the slash in his back, and Leah was pressing it firmly against the deepest part. Anthony and Eric had turned back to their Lycan forms, and they and Lupe were crammed into the front seat next to Hank.

"Where are we?" Leah asked. The female Lycan had a nasty looking gash across her forehead, and she pressed the blood-soaked material against Jack's back when he shifted into Lycan form. He was still unconscious, and Amelia stroked his soft fur as Hank stopped in front of the farmhouse.

"Amelia? Where are we?" Hank's ordinarily ruddy face was completely white, and he looked like he was about to vomit.

"Get him out of the truck! Hurry!" Amelia threw open the back door and slipped out, easing Jack's head onto the seat.

She bolted for the front door as it opened, and Luna came bounding out, barking loudly. Joanna stepped out onto the porch. Flour covered her hands and the front of the red apron she wore.

"Amelia?" She frowned at the sight of Amelia in just her bra and jeans. "My love, what's wrong? What happened to your cheek?"

"Joanna, you have to help us. It's Jack," Amelia gasped out, climbing the steps of the porch and grabbing her birth mother's hands in her gloved ones. "He's been hurt badly."

Joanna's eyes widened as she glanced behind Amelia. Hank wore just his pants, and the three other Lycans were completely naked. An equally naked Jack, covered in blood and supported between the four of them, was still shifting back and forth between his Lycan form and his human form.

"Joanna, please help him. Please," Amelia said.

"Bring him into the house – quickly," Joanna said.

CHAPTER 20

"These will be too big, I'm afraid, but they're better than nothing." Joanna handed the pile of clothing to Leah.

Wrapped a blanket from the couch, Leah smiled her thanks.

"There are some pants and shirts for those two as well. They'll probably be too small. My husband wasn't nearly as tall as either of them." Joanna pointed to Anthony and Eric, who'd shifted back to their Lycan form. Luna sat between them and Lupe, panting happily and looking from wolf to wolf. She seemed both delighted and confused by the added canines in the house. Lupe lay motionless on the floor with his head on his paws, not moving even when Luna licked the top of his head.

"We appreciate your kindness," Leah said. "Will he live?"

Joanna nodded. "I think so. I couldn't heal him completely. His wounds were severe, and my abilities do not seem to be as effective with your kind."

She stared down at her hands. "I don't understand why they aren't as effective, but they were enough to keep him alive. It could take weeks for him to heal completely or only days. Being a half-breed means there's no guarantee that he'll even heal fully. I'm going to start dinner. I'm assuming you'll be staying the night?"

Leah cleared her throat. "We don't wish to be a burden on you. It's probably better if we leave."

Joanna frowned. "Amelia and Hank told me that you protected Jack from your pack. I may not know much about the Lycans, but what you did has ostracized you from your pack. Where will you go?"

Anthony shifted to his human form and joined them. "She's right, Leah. We have nowhere else to go." He dressed quickly in the clothes Joanna had provided and then ran his fingers over the gash on Leah's forehead.

"It's fine." She smiled reassuringly at him. "It's starting to heal."

He kissed her cheek, and Leah turned to Joanna. "Could I help you with dinner?"

"Sure," Joanna said. "Let me show you to the bathroom first. You can get dressed, and if you'd like, I'll try to heal that gash on your head."

They left, and Anthony glanced at Eric. His younger brother shifted and started to dress.

"What do we do, Anthony? Where do we go? We cannot stay with the human forever," he said.

Anthony sighed wearily. "I do not know, brother."

"We shouldn't have defied David. Now we have no pack!" Eric's voice rose, and his entire body rippled and shook.

"Calm yourself, Eric." Anthony clapped a hand on the back of his neck and squeezed lightly. "David has gone mad – you know this. It's better to separate ourselves from his madness. Besides, you, Leah and I are still a pack."

When Eric didn't reply, Anthony squeezed his neck again. "We will figure this out, little brother. I promise you."

* * *

"AMELIA, WE CAN'T STAY HERE." HANK STOOD BY THE BEDROOM window, staring into the growing darkness.

Amelia sat cross-legged on the bed beside Jack's sleeping body and rubbed his arm. "They don't know we're here, Hank. We can stay for a few days to let Jack heal a bit more before we try to move him."

"This is a small town, and people will talk. The Lycans will find us, probably within a day or two, if not from the gossip, then just by our smell. We need to leave this place."

"Where do we go?" she asked.

He turned to face her. "My parent's home. Jack can heal, and we'll figure out what to do."

"What about Leah and Anthony and Eric?"

He shrugged. "I don't care what they do."

She stroked Jack's face. "We have to take them with us, Hank."

"No, Amelia."

"Yes," she insisted. "You said it yourself – they were protecting Jack. They can't go back to their pack now. Where else are they going to go?"

"Amelia…"

"They're coming with us, Hank. Either we all go, or I'm staying here."

"Are you crazy? You can't stay here!" Hank said.

She stiffened her back. "Just try to make me leave."

"Amelia," Hank ran his hand through his hair, "I can't let you stay here. If – when Jack wakes up, he'll kill me for leaving you behind."

She kissed Jack's cool forehead and smiled at Hank. "Then I guess all of us are leaving."

* * *

"No, Mom. I don't know when I'm coming home. Listen, I know it's hard to understand, but I can't tell you where I am." Amelia rubbed her forehead. "I know you're worried, but I'm fine. I'm with Jack, and Ray is working to find out who broke into my house."

She gripped the phone tight to her ear. "I know, Mom. I love you, and I'll see you soon, okay? Give my love to Dad."

She ended the call and rubbed again at her forehead. She had been nauseous all morning and couldn't remember the last time she felt so tired.

"Amelia?" Joy's soft voice spoke behind her, and she turned, forcing herself to smile at Jack's mother.

"Hi, Joy."

"Hi. I brought you some tea. It will help settle your stomach."

"Thank you. You're very kind."

Joy handed her the cup of tea, carefully avoiding touching Amelia even through her gloves. Amelia smiled a little. One good thing about getting involved with Lycans was their willingness to accept any and all weirdness.

It had been nearly two weeks since they'd crept from Joanna's house like thieves in the night. They'd appeared on Joy's and Tom's doorstep just before dawn. The three Lycans agreed to go with them, although Amelia was confident that Anthony and Eric agreed to go only because of Leah.

Over the last week or so, the outcast Lycans and Jack's family had begun to bond. Amelia was surprised at how quickly they formed a connection. Joy, in particular, was thrilled to have other Lycans in the house. Her enthusiasm and genuine warmth had quickly won over the three Lycans.

"You should lie down for a while, Amelia. You'll feel better." Leah joined them, studying Amelia's carefully. "Your worry for your mate has worn you out."

Amelia could feel the heat rising in her cheeks. Everyone in the house, including Jack's parents, had referred to her as Jack's mate since they'd arrived. At first, she'd been too worried about Jack to bother correcting them, and now she didn't know how to tell them. It felt awkward to blurt out that she wasn't with Jack and that he refused to entertain the idea of taking her as his mate.

She sighed inwardly. When he woke, Jack would tell them himself. Tears threatened, and she blinked them back fiercely. Once his family and the others found out she was not Jack's mate, they would be angry with her. It was her fault that Jack had nearly died and that Anthony and his family were ousted from their pack. Her pulse thudded, and nausea increased as a new thought occurred to her.

What if they were so angry they made her leave? Jack's parents were kind, but their child had almost died because of her. Lycans protected their pack, and their belief that she was Jack's mate meant they had taken her in without hesitation. But once they knew the truth...

Jack wouldn't let them kick you out. A small voice in her head tried to reassure her, but another immediately crowded it out.

He's made it clear that he will never take you as his mate. You knew what this was from the beginning. Hell, he only slept with you because you threw yourself at him repeatedly. Do you honestly think he'll want anything to do with you after this? His kind nearly tore him apart because of you. He'll tell them the truth when he wakes, and you need to accept it. In the meantime, put your damn big girl panties on and figure out what you're going to do and where you're going to go.

She took a deep, shuddering breath as Leah took her gloved hand in her bare one and squeezed it lightly. "Amelia? Are you okay?"

"Yes. Just tired, I think. I'll do what you suggested and lie down with Jack. I'll come down later to help with supper."

Joy shook her head. "Don't be silly. Leah will help me with dinner. Won't you, love?"

Leah nodded. "Yes. How much sleep have you gotten in the last week, Amelia?"

Amelia shrugged but didn't reply. Her worry for Jack, her growing embarrassment at pretending to be Jack's mate when she wasn't, and a surprisingly large bout of homesickness for her small house had kept her from sleeping well.

"Get some rest, Amelia. I'll bring a tray up to you later, okay?" Leah squeezed her hand again.

"Thank you, Leah." Tears threatening again, Amelia hurried from the room before Leah and Joy could see them.

* * *

LEAH SAT DOWN NEXT TO JOY ON THE COUCH. SHE REPEATEDLY tapped her fingers on her thigh before deciding to say it. Joy had likely already picked up on it as well, right? "Amelia's scent has changed."

"I know. I noticed it this morning when she came downstairs," Joy said.

"Have the others noticed?"

Joy laughed. "Of course not. And they won't. She is not their mate, and it is too subtle of a change for men to pay much attention. It'll be at least a month before they even notice it."

She stood and picked up Amelia's abandoned tea mug. "When Jack wakes, he'll notice the scent change. She's his mate – how could he not? Of course, if he's anything like a full Lycan, he won't understand what it means. They never understand what their mate's scent change means with the first pup. He'll feel more protective of her, more anxious to claim her as his own in front of others, but nothing more."

"Do you think she knows?" Leah followed Joy out of the kitchen.

"No. It's still much too early. But she'll realize soon enough. In the meantime, we need to encourage her to rest."

CHAPTER 21

Amelia's eyelids fluttered up, and she stared at the ceiling in the dark bedroom. What had woken her up? Something was different, but it was hard to think past the weariness. She rubbed her eyes and stared at the alarm clock. It was just after two in the morning, and she scrubbed her hand across her face. Had she been dreaming? She couldn't remember dreaming, but...

She sat up straight, her heartbeat suddenly racing out of control. She'd grown so used to hearing Jack's steady breathing that it had taken her a minute to realize it was missing. Fear gnawing at her belly, she stared at the empty spot in the bed next to her. Fear and hope clamouring in her belly, she threw back the covers. Where was he? Two hours ago, when she had finally drifted off to sleep, he'd still been unconscious.

The bedroom door opened, and a pale, shaky-looking Jack entered the room. Lupe was at his heels, and the wolf could hardly contain his glee. He pranced around Jack's legs, whining softly, licking, and nipping at Jack's hands until Jack patted his head.

"Quiet, Lupe. You'll wake the others," he muttered.

"Jack!" Amelia nearly fell out of bed before running across the room. She hesitated in front of him. She wanted to hug him, but he stared at her strangely, his nostrils flaring as he inhaled deeply.

"Jack, are you – how do you feel?" she asked.

He didn't reply at first, just continued to give her an odd look.

"Jack? What's wrong?" She crossed her arms over her torso, feeling weird and self-conscious. Why was he staring at her like that?

His face smoothed out, and he smiled at her. "Good. Tired, but good."

"Thank God. I was so worried about you."

She was still desperate to hug him but settled for awkwardly patting his arm. He was acting so strangely she didn't know what to say or do. He frowned and reached out for her, his arms wrapping around her waist to pull her up against him. He buried his face in her neck and squeezed her tightly.

She returned his hug, stupid hot tears sliding down her cheeks as she stroked his back. "Where were you?"

"The bathroom," he murmured against her throat. "I'm sorry I woke you."

"I'm not." She stared up at him. "I've missed you."

"I missed you too." He cupped her face and kissed her lightly as Lupe tried to squeeze his large body between them.

She laughed through her tears. "You shouldn't be out of bed. Come on."

She led him back to the bed, and he collapsed on it with a soft sigh as she turned on the bedside lamp. As Lupe jumped on the bed and lay beside him, she carefully peeled back the white bandage covering his side.

She sucked in her breath. Two days ago, the formerly

gaping wound had been a long and jagged cut, and his side was still swollen and red. Now, only a large scar ran from above his left hipbone and around to the middle of his back.

"My God," she breathed. "I can't believe it."

He shrugged. "We're fast healers."

"It's been two weeks," she said.

"What? Are you serious?" he stared at her, his face slack with shock.

"Yes. Jack – you nearly died. Do you remember what happened?"

He nodded. "Yeah, most of it. The leader of the Lycans who live in your town has gone mad."

"Yes. Leah said that it's been happening gradually, but -"

"Leah?"

"She's Anthony's mate. He's the Lycan with the scar, and Eric, the redhead, is his brother. The three of them helped you and protected you from their pack until Hank and Lupe found you."

"Why?"

"They know that David has gone mad. They said he ordered you killed like it meant nothing," Amelia said.

"He wants you for himself. He wants to mate with you in the hopes that your children would be Lycans with your power," he said hoarsely.

"I know. Anthony told me."

She couldn't stop the tears or the trembling. "We took you to Joanna, and she did what she could to help you. She couldn't heal you completely, but she saved your life. Then we drove here to your parents. We needed to get out of town, and Hank insisted we bring you here. I think – I think he was worried that you were going to die, and he wanted your parents to see you."

"Climb into bed with me, Amelia." Jack tugged on her hand, and she climbed over him, pushing Lupe to the far side of the bed so she could crawl under the covers and curl up against Jack.

"Lupe, get down," Jack said.

The wolf ignored him, curling up into a ball and resting his large head on Amelia's hip. He stared adoringly at Jack.

"Lupe, down," Jack said again.

"Let him stay," Amelia said. "I don't mind, and he's missed you as much as I have."

Jack put his arm around her, and she rested her head on his broad chest as he rubbed and petted Lupe's head. The wolf made a distinctly human-like sigh and closed his eyes.

"Are you hungry?" Amelia asked.

Jack shook his head. "No. Just very tired."

"I'm so sorry, Jack."

"For what?"

"This is my fault. You almost died because of me."

He rubbed her back with his warm hand. "This isn't your fault, Amelia. Do you understand?"

She didn't reply as he yawned tiredly. She rubbed her hand through the hair on his chest. "Go to sleep, my love."

"Yeah, sleep," he muttered. Already, he was starting to drift off, his breathing deepening and his arm relaxing around her. She kissed his chest and stared into the darkness, listening to the solid beat of his heart. Jack was awake. Tomorrow, his family and the others would discover the truth about her, and she would never see him again. She wanted to cry, but she blinked the tears back this time. She would not waste her final night with him by crying like a silly little girl.

* * *

"I owe you my life." Jack stared solemnly at Anthony.

Amelia stood nervously by the bed. It was late afternoon,

and the difference between how he looked last night and now was incredible. It was as though Jack's healing powers had kicked into high gear. He'd spent most of the morning with his parents and Hank. They'd crowded into the bedroom as soon as Amelia told them Jack was awake, and she'd slipped out of the room unnoticed.

She'd gone to the impressive flower garden that Tom was cultivating in their backyard, sat on the small stone bench, and waited for Tom, Joy, or Hank to find her and tell her to leave. One of them would refer to her as Jack's mate, she was sure of it, and Jack would tell them the truth.

The minutes had ticked by, then an hour and then another until finally, her stomach rolling with nausea and feeling faint from worry and nerves, she'd stretched out on the soft grass. Her sleepless night caught up with her, and despite her fear, she fell asleep.

Leah woke her an hour later. Jack was looking for her, and Amelia followed Leah into the house. She climbed the stairs with dread in her belly and peeked into Jack's room. His warm smile sent relief shooting through her. She'd joined him on the bed, feeling like she'd dodged a bullet. A few minutes later, Joy brought a food tray for lunch to the room, enough for her and Jack to share.

"Where have you been all morning?" Jack asked.

"I thought you should spend some time with your family without me hanging around," she said.

"I like it when you hang around." He rubbed her thigh, and a ribbon of desire had twisted through her. It'd been two weeks since they'd had sex, and she was ashamed to admit how much she wanted to have him between her legs again. He had nearly died and was still healing, and she couldn't stop wishing he'd fuck her. When he continued to rub her thigh, she ignored the desire in her belly and tried to concentrate on the food in front of her. She had nibbled on the crackers but left her soup untouched.

"You're not eating your soup," Jack said disapprovingly.

"I'm not that hungry." She couldn't tell him she was too nervous and sad to eat.

"You need to eat more," he insisted. "You look worn out."

"Gee, thanks. You're good for a girl's ego," she teased lightly.

After lunch, they'd napped together, and neither objected when Lupe crowded onto the bed with them again.

Now, Jack sat in the overstuffed armchair by the window as he and Anthony stared at each other.

"David has gone mad. He should never have ordered our pack to kill you," Anthony said.

The door opened before Jack could reply, and Leah and Eric stepped into the room. Jack was up and out of the chair so quickly that it hit the back of the wall with a loud thud. He crossed to the bed and yanked Amelia behind his broad body.

"Jack, what's wrong?"

Jack growled deep in his throat. Amelia blinked in confusion as Jack's body swelled and the hair thickened on his face and body. Lupe stalked over on stiff legs and joined Jack in growling.

"Easy, my friend." Anthony took a step forward and held up his hands. He glanced behind him and frowned. "Leah, enough."

Leah stood in front of Eric, her eyes a brilliant green as she snarled softly under her breath. She glanced at Anthony, and he briefly shook his head before returning to Jack.

"My brother won't harm your mate. I give you my word," he said.

Shit. Amelia couldn't help the little jolt her body made when Anthony called her Jack's mate. Thankfully, Jack hadn't seemed to notice. But the way his body continued to swell sent little bolts of alarm up and down her spine.

She stood in front of him and cupped his face. "Jack? Please calm down."

He ignored her and bared his teeth at Eric. His fangs had dropped, and when he spoke, his voice had roughened until it was barely recognizable as his. "You will stay away from her, pup. I will tear out your throat if I even catch you sniffing her scent. Do I make myself clear?"

"Jack!" Amelia squeezed his arms hard, and he finally looked at her. He was dangerously close to shifting, and she cupped his face again. "Stop this. Please. He saved your life as well."

With a loud snarl, Jack shook free of her and turned around. He stared out the window, his fists clenching and unclenching as Amelia rubbed his back. After nearly five minutes, he turned back to them.

"He was acting under David's orders," Anthony said. "My brother would never have tried to take her if our pack leader had not ordered him to do so."

Jack didn't reply, and Amelia slipped her arm around his waist. "Eric apologized to me, and I've accepted it. We're friends now."

She smiled at Eric, and he smiled tentatively in return. Jack immediately growled and stiffened against her.

"Jack, it's okay," she said, rubbing his back again.

"You are not to touch her. Do you understand?" Jack said to Eric.

Eric nodded as Amelia squeezed Jack's waist, suddenly worried that his near-death experience had rattled his brain. "Jack, I won't let anyone touch me but you. You know that."

Jack pulled her even closer and gave Anthony a hard look. "You're not to touch her either. She's mine."

Disbelief washed over Amelia. Keeping her voice soft and

low, she said, "Leah is Anthony's mate. He has no interest in me. What is going on with you?"

She stared up at Jack. She knew he was protective of her. She knew he could be possessive but was entirely unprepared for his extreme reaction to the other Lycans. Was this normal behaviour when a pack of Lycans were together? Jack had returned to normal size, but his eyes were still a bright jade, and she could feel his big body vibrating against hers. Lupe continued to growl softly.

The door opened, and Hank stuck his head in the room. "Hey, Mom says that dinner is ready."

He took one look at Jack's angry face and strode into the room. The floor shook slightly under his feet as he looked distrustfully at Anthony and the others before taking Amelia's gloved hand. "Amelia, what's -"

With an angry roar, Jack shoved Hank as hard as he could. Lupe made a startled yelp, and Amelia cried out as Hank staggered back but didn't fall.

"What the hell, Jack?" he snapped.

"She is mine!" Jack snarled at him. He pushed Amelia behind him and then stalked toward Hank, growling low in his chest.

"Calm down, you idiot!" Hank said. "I know she's yours. Jesus Christ, what the hell is wrong with you?"

"I see how you look at her," Jack said softly. "Did you think I wouldn't notice?"

Hank's eyes glowed, and the shirt buttons strained at his chest. "Watch your tone, little brother. I handed your ass to you on the regular when we were children. I can still do so now."

"Go ahead and try," Jack snarled.

The two men circled each other in the small bedroom. Amelia started forward, and Leah grabbed her gloved arm. "No, Amelia. Don't get between them."

"Let me go." She tugged at Leah's hand. "I have to stop them."

Leah refused to release her. "No. You're human and don't understand the Lycan way. Trust me – they will work it out themselves."

"You're acting like a spoiled child," Hank growled. "We all know she is your mate. You don't have to be such an asshole about it."

Jack bared his teeth at him in response, and Hank scowled. "Fine. You want to do this? Let's do it. It's been many years since I have taught you a lesson in respect, little brother."

He and Jack started toward each other as dismay flooded through Amelia. Before they could attack each other, their father stepped into the room. He took one look at them before stepping between them and pushing them both back. His sons dwarfed Tom, but he glared fearlessly at them. "What's going on in here?"

"Jack's being an asshole," Hank said.

"He touched Amelia," Jack huffed.

"Seriously, you two?" Tom said. "You're both grown adults. Act like it."

"He started it. Spoiled little brat," Hank said.

With another soft roar, Jack lunged forward. Hank bared his fangs and reached for Jack.

Tom shoved Jack back in a surprising show of strength before turning to Hank. Hank towered over his father, but when Tom pushed him hard on the chest and shouted, "Enough!" the massive Lycan cowered in front of him.

Tom turned and glared at Jack. "Your brother is not after Amelia, and you know that. How often have I told you to use your head, Jack?" He tapped Jack on the temple. "Stop letting your emotions rule you. Do you hear me?"

"Yes, Dad," Jack muttered.

ELIZABETH KELLY

Hank snorted laughter, and Tom turned on him. "This is funny to you? Your brother nearly died. He's still not fully healed, and I come in here to find you picking a fight with him. Have you gone mad?"

"Sorry, Dad." Hank dropped his gaze to the floor, his face bright red.

"Neither of you are teenagers. Stop acting like you are." Tom glared at both before smoothing his hair back and adjusting his shirt. "I won't tell your mother about this. You know how she hates it when you fight."

He walked to the door and stared at everyone. "Dinner is ready. I expect all of you to be on your best behaviour. Your mother and Leah worked hard on this meal, and you'll be respectful and polite to each other."

His gaze landed on his sons. "Do you understand?"

"Yes, sir," Jack and Hank said in unison.

"Good." Tom left the room, and Leah broke the tension by giggling loudly.

"That was awesome. I've never seen Lycans submit to a human before. The looks on your faces..."

She snorted and hiccupped and tried to hold back the laughter, but her small frame shook. "Anthony, did you see him? They outweigh him by, like, a hundred pounds, and he wasn't even afraid of them."

She turned to Jack and Hank, whose faces were both bright red.

"Your dad is a badass," she said.

Her emotions whiplashing back and forth, Amelia tried not to smile. It *had* been funny to see Hank and Jack, two of the bravest and biggest men she knew, be so thoroughly chastised by their dad. She looked at Leah and couldn't stop the laughter from spilling out. Leah, whose giggles had just started to taper off, burst into loud laughter again.

Anthony and Eric grinned, and Lupe made a soft 'woof',

his tail wagging madly. Jack stepped forward and stuck out his hand to Hank. His eyes had returned to their usual golden brown, and an odd mixture of shame and amusement was on his face.

"I'm sorry, Hank." He glanced briefly at Amelia. "I don't know what's wrong with me."

Hank nodded and pulled him into a hug, clapping his back hard. Jack winced but returned his hug.

CHAPTER 22

A melia climbed into the bed beside Jack. He pulled her into his embrace, and she curled into his solid warmth. She tried to ignore the desire that went through her when Jack rested his hand on her hip.

"Are you tired, Amelia?" he asked.

"A little." She smiled up at him. "How are you feeling?"

"Fine. Still a little tired, but it's better than it was this morning."

"Good."

He moved his hand, and she gasped when it brushed against her ass. Her pelvis was throbbing with that now familiar ache, and she shifted her lower body away from his.

"What's wrong?" he asked.

"Nothing." She reached up and gave him a quick, chaste kiss. "Good night, Jack."

He frowned again and twisted onto his side until he faced her. He cupped her face and kissed her slowly and thoroughly. "Tell me what's wrong."

"Nothing," she repeated. Her nipples hardened inside her t-shirt, and she pushed away from him, afraid he would feel them against his chest. He needed rest, not sex. Maybe it would be better if she slept on the couch tonight.

"There's something wrong, and I want to know what it is." He hauled her back against him, and when his hand cupped her ass, she was helpless to stop her small moan of pleasure.

"Tell me," Jack said.

"Fine," she said irritably. "You almost died, and you're still healing, and all I can think about is fucking you."

She blushed immediately, but Jack grinned at her. "Thank God. I've been dying to touch you since this morning, but you seemed distant, and I wasn't sure if…."

He suddenly kissed her hard, pushing his tongue between her lips. She returned his kiss eagerly until a little of her common sense returned. She pulled back and stared up at him. "Jack, we can't. You're still healing."

"I'm healed." He nuzzled her neck, kissing her soft skin before nipping lightly at it.

"No, you're not," she said. "You're better, but you're still tired and weak. I know you are."

"Then I guess you'll just have to do all the work," he breathed into her ear.

"What do you mean?" She arched her back when he traced her ear with his tongue.

He shifted onto his back and pulled her on top of him. He slid his hands under her t-shirt and cupped her bare breasts, kneading them gently. "I mean, I'm going to lay here and let you have your dirty way with me."

Her giggle turned into a soft sigh of pleasure when he ran his thumbs over her nipples. She sat up, straddling his hips and rubbing herself against his erection before peeling off her t-shirt and dropping it to the floor.

It landed on Lupe's head, and he made a soft snort of

displeasure, shaking it off and moving to the far corner of the room.

"Sorry, Lupe." She laughed and turned back to Jack. The laughter died in her throat at the look on his face. He was staring at her bare breasts, and the heat in his gaze was enough to turn her nipples into tight, stiff peaks. When he brushed his thumbs over them again, she moaned his name before pushing his hands away.

"Don't move, Jack. I'm doing all the work, remember?" she said teasingly.

He dropped his hands to his sides and groaned under his breath when she leaned over him and brushed the tips of her breasts against his hard chest. She kissed his collarbone before moving down his chest. He bucked against her when she ran her tongue over his flat nipple and then sucked it into her mouth.

She moved down his body, licking and sucking and exploring his warm skin. When she traced his new scar with the tip of her tongue, he groaned so loudly she gave him a look of alarm.

"Jack, shh. The others will hear."

He nodded his agreement and clamped his mouth shut as she placed warm, wet kisses across his scar before trailing down to his hip bone and nipping at it lightly. Her breasts pressed against his dick, and he rubbed himself against her, groaning again when one stiff nipple brushed across the tip. She smiled at the look of need on his face and pushed herself down his body until her mouth hovered over his swollen cock. She licked just the tip and then blew lightly on it. He gathered fistfuls of the sheets and uttered a curse under his breath.

She licked him again, tracing the head with her wet tongue, and he looked at her pleadingly. "Amelia, please."

She smiled and slid her mouth down over his cock. He

gasped and thrust his hips upward. She held the base of his cock and licked him from base to tip like he was a lollipop before taking him into her mouth again. She had no idea what she was doing, but she must have been something right based on the moans and sighs above her.

She began to experiment, rubbing his cock in her loosely clasped fist as she slid her mouth up and down. She kissed his inner thighs and then gently cupped his balls in her hand, marvelling at their heaviness, before giving his hard shaft another slow lick.

His hands threaded through her hair, and she smiled when he urged her mouth back to his cock. She took just the head of him into her mouth and sucked hard, rubbing her tongue along the underside as she did.

"Oh my God! Amelia, stop!" he muttered. She ignored him and continued to suck as he arched his hips against her repeatedly. He pushed her away, and she released his cock with a soft pop.

She shimmied out of her panties and then scooted up his body until her mouth was at his ear. She reached down and stroked his cock with firm pulls of her hand. "Why did you make me stop, Jack? Didn't you like having your cock in my mouth?"

His hands tightened on her hips. "I was too close. If you'd kept doing that, I would have come in your mouth."

"Would you like that?" she asked. "Would you like to come in my mouth?"

"Jesus Christ," he groaned.

"Would you?" she asked again. Her usual shyness had disappeared, and she revelled in her newfound power of making Jack want her this much.

He hesitated and then nodded. "Yes, I'd like that."

"Good." She tried to move down his body, and he grabbed her shoulders and pulled her back.

She pouted at him. "I thought you said you'd like it."

He lifted his head and sucked on her lower lip. "I would - just not this time. I want to be inside you, Amelia."

She smiled and straddled him, brushing her pelvis against him before she reached between them and took his cock into her hand again. She guided it towards her warm opening, sighing with frustration when she couldn't get the correct angle.

Before Jack could help her, she crouched over him and tried again. This time when she placed his cock at her opening, he slid easily into her. She sank down, sheathing him entirely inside of her, and rested her knees on either side of his hips. She waited as she stretched around him, watching Jack's face as he panted beneath her.

He reached up and cupped her breasts as she continued to straddle him. "Amelia, please," he said through gritted teeth.

"Please, what, Jack?" She smiled at him, and he tugged on both her nipples, forcing a groan of pleasure from her throat.

He moved his hands to her hips and thrust into her. She immediately leaned forward and let him slip out of her. "Hey, I thought I was supposed to do all the work?"

"Oh, God." He breathed deeply as she rubbed her breasts against his chest.

"Promise me you'll be good, and I'll ride your cock again," she said.

"I'll be good," he said.

"Promise?"

"I promise. Please, Amelia."

She was secretly delighted by his begging, and she reached behind her and slipped his cock back into her pussy. This time, there was no need to wait for her to adjust. She was wet and slick and so turned on that just the feel of his cock filling her up nearly made her come.

She braced her hands on his chest and bounced up and

down enthusiastically, watching his face carefully. When his eyes lightened to green, she stopped moving and leaned over to kiss him. He kissed her hard on the mouth, his pelvis rocking gently beneath her, and she nipped at his bottom lip.

"Is that being good?" she asked.

He glared at her, his eyes glowing in the darkness, and clamped hard hands around her waist. "If you don't start moving right now, I swear to God, I will push you up against the wall and fuck you until you come so hard you scream, Amelia. I don't care who hears it."

His words made her muscles clench around him in a spasm of pleasure, and his cock was suddenly drenched in her juices. She flushed with embarrassment, and he grinned wickedly at her before cupping the back of her neck. He nipped at her neck and then her mouth before whispering, "Fuck me, Amelia."

She let her hips rise and fall against him. He licked at her mouth, and she opened it so he could slide his tongue inside. He met her thrust for thrust, his hands moving to her waist and holding her tightly.

"Jack, oh Jack," she whimpered, her hands digging into this broad chest. She'd forgotten about teasing him, forgotten that she was in charge. She wanted the pleasure that only Jack could give her.

He increased the speed, and she met each of his pounding thrusts eagerly. He pushed his hand between their bodies and rubbed her clit. She stiffened, and a small cry escaped from her mouth. As she came apart around him, he grabbed her hips and arched his back, making his own cry of pleasure as he climaxed deep inside of her.

* * *

"FOR A HALF-BREED, YOUR MATE IS A QUICK HEALER." LEAH smiled at Amelia as they cleared the breakfast dishes. Amelia twitched and automatically looked behind her for Jack, which was silly because Jack wasn't even home. He'd healed completely in the week and a half since he'd finally woke. He'd returned to work, leaving Amelia with his parents and Anthony, Leah, and Eric during the day.

It was so strange to realize that she had been living alone, hiding from people and resigned to a lonely life just over a month ago. The last two weeks had passed by like a dream. She spent her days visiting with Joy and Leah and helping around the house. She'd soaked up their friendship like a plant dying of thirst. She'd even bonded with Tom. He'd been delighted to discover she loved plants and she spent many hours in his flower garden with him. Being around Jack's family and being accepted for what she was made her realize how lonely and miserable she'd been.

Her nights were even more pleasant. She wasn't sure if this was a Lycan thing, and she wasn't comfortable enough with Leah to ask her, but Jack seemed insatiable to her. They had sex every night, sometimes more than once, and he'd begun to teach her all of the ways they could show each other pleasure.

She was an eager student. Her need for him seemed to rival his need for her. Even when things went wrong – like last night when she attempted to ride him backward and fell off his lap and onto the floor in a graceless heap - she felt very little embarrassment. He had picked her up, the worry dropping from his face when he had seen how hard she was giggling and set her back in his lap before kissing away her giggles.

Afterwards, they shared stories about their childhoods and other small insignificant details. He collected old books - she loved to dance. He couldn't stand the smell of lilacs - her favourite colour was pink. He told her about the first girl he fell in love with. He had never told her he was half-Lycan, and although he knew there was no future for them, he had still been heartbroken when she dumped him after high school. She talked about Richard, how funny and silly he'd been, and how much she still missed him.

They never spoke of the future. They hadn't even talked about David's obsession with her or what to do about it. They couldn't stay with his parents forever. Despite Joy's obvious enthusiasm for having a pack of Lycans in the house, it was too small of a place for all of them. Besides, Anthony, Leah, and Eric grew more restless by the day. They wanted to return to their home, and if Amelia was honest with herself, she also wanted to return.

They would have to talk about it sooner or later, but the last two weeks had been so wonderful - a perfect bubble of good days and even better nights - that she couldn't bring herself to talk about it to Jack. She knew the sweet cloud of perfection surrounding them would dissipate when she brought it up. She didn't want it to. She wanted to pretend that it would last forever. Jack never mentioned it to her, either. She had a feeling that Anthony had spoken with him about it, but Jack didn't share any of their conversations with her, and she hadn't asked.

She sighed and scraped some leftover egg into the garbage, ignoring the queasiness in her stomach. The others still referred to her as Jack's mate, and, to her surprise, Jack hadn't corrected them. Maybe he thought of her as his mate now.

Fat chance.

Her inner voice was painfully blunt. If she weren't such a chickenshit, she'd ask him straight out if he considered her to be his mate. She had tried a couple of times, but each time, the memory of that morning in front of her house, when he had told her in no uncertain terms that he could never be her mate, came crashing back to her, and she lost her nerve.

He was only being kind, she decided. He wasn't correcting the others because he knew his family would kick her out for nearly getting him killed.

Also, that familiar, vicious little voice deep inside her head spoke up, *let's not forget that you're spreading your legs for him every night. When he grows tired of you, and he will, what do you think will happen to you then? Where will you go? You've undoubtedly lost your job by now. You can't go back home, and even if you could, your parents and Ray are confused and upset that you won't tell them where you are. Do you think they would just welcome you back with open arms?*

"Amelia?" Leah touched her gloved arm tentatively. "Are you okay?"

"Yeah." Amelia placed a hand on her stomach. "I just can't seem to kick this stomach bug."

Leah gave her a strange look, but before Amelia could question her, the smell of the uneaten eggs wafted to her again, and her stomach lurched alarmingly. She pushed past Leah and ran to the bathroom. She threw up her entire breakfast and then dry heaved for a few minutes more. She flushed the toilet and closed the lid before raising her knees and resting her head on them. Her stomach was still rolling and twisting with nausea, and she wasn't entirely sure that she wasn't going to vomit again.

A gentle hand fell on her neck, and she stiffened as Leah's thoughts flooded through her mind. Leah grunted with surprise and stumbled back, staring wide-eyed at Amelia.

"I'm sorry, Amelia. I forgot that I shouldn't touch you."

Amelia stared at Leah. "Why would you be thinking that?"

"Thinking what?" Leah asked.

"I'm not pregnant." Amelia cupped her elbows with trembling hands. "I'm on the pill."

Leah crouched beside her. "When is the moon full for you?"

Amelia stared blankly at her. "I don't understand what you mean."

"Your monthlies, Amelia. When are you due to bleed?"

"I – um, my cycle starts on the tenth."

"Today is the seventeenth," Leah said.

"That's not possible. It can't be that late."

"It is," Leah said.

"I am not pregnant, Leah." Amelia's voice rose, and Leah made a soothing gesture without touching her. "I'm on the pill. It's just the stress and the worry about what happened, that's all."

"Amelia, you're pregnant. Your scent has changed. Both Joy and I noticed it weeks ago," Leah said.

Hoo boy, Leah had lost her marbles.

Hoping her smile didn't completely scream, 'You're freaking crazy, lady', Amelia said, "What do you mean, my scent has changed?"

"It's a Lycan thing. When a woman is with child, her scent changes. Lycans can smell the change. Yours has changed."

"Jack would have noticed, and he hasn't said anything to me." Amelia could hear the hysteria in her voice.

"He has noticed," Leah said. "He just doesn't understand what it means. Male Lycans are not as attuned to the subtle changes. Do you remember that day in the bedroom when he nearly attacked his brother for touching you?"

Amelia nodded.

"He was reacting to your scent change. On a subconscious level, he knows you're carrying his pup. It's what caused him to react to the other Lycans. It's in his blood to protect his mate and his pups."

"I'm not his mate," Amelia said.

Leah frowned. "What do you mean?"

"I mean, I'm not his mate. Just before he was attacked, he told me that he would never take me as his mate. He said that Lycans were not meant to mate with humans, and he wouldn't turn me into an outcast like he is."

"But his birth parents and his adoptive parents…."

"It's the reason he's so adamant against it. He believes that his birth father regrets leaving his pack and that Joy is, deep down, miserable without a pack. He doesn't want me to be an outcast among my kind, even though I told him I already am," Amelia said.

Amelia rubbed at her stomach. "I didn't say anything to anyone while he was healing because I was afraid his family would make me leave if they found out. Their child, their brother, nearly died because of me. And then when he woke, I didn't know what to do, but Jack hasn't corrected them either."

Leah smiled at her. "That's because he is in love with you. He considers you to be his mate."

"No, Leah. You're mistaken. He hasn't told his family about not being his mate because he is kind and knows I have nowhere else to go." She hesitated and, cheeks flushing, looked at the floor. "And because we're sleeping together. But eventually, he'll tire of me, and then he'll ask me to leave."

"He won't, Amelia. I get that I don't know him very well, but he doesn't strike me as the kind of Lycan who will abandon the woman carrying his pup."

Amelia stood abruptly, swallowing back nausea as Leah stood next to her.

"Amelia, where are you going?"

"To the pharmacy." She gave Leah an almost apologetic look. "I'm going to buy a pregnancy test and prove to you that it's the stomach flu."

CHAPTER 23

"Amelia? Why are you out here by yourself?" Jack's deep voice caressed her a moment before his arms did. He folded her into his embrace, his muscular chest against her back, and kissed the top of her head.

She stared at the flowers around her. "I like being in the garden. It's peaceful here."

"Yeah, it is. It was one of my favourite places as a child."

Jack's hands were clasped around her belly, and Amelia placed her trembling hands on them.

"You didn't eat much supper," Jack said.

"I wasn't hungry," she said.

He nuzzled her neck. "Honey, will you tell me what's wrong?"

"I'm pregnant."

He stiffened behind her, and she clung to his hands before allowing him to pull away.

She wiped the tears from her cheeks and turned to face him. He was staring at her in shock, his usually tanned face pale. "Are you – are you sure?"

She nodded. "Yes. I've been feeling sick in the mornings,

and Leah told me my scent had changed. She said that it had changed because I was with child."

He shoved his hands into his pockets. "That's an old Lycan's tale, Amelia. We can't tell when a woman is pregnant, Leah is being -"

"I took a pregnancy test," she said. "It was positive. I'm pregnant."

"But you're on the pill, aren't you?"

She nodded. "Yes. I don't know what happened. Either I forgot to take one and have forgotten that I forgot, or someone at the pill factory fell asleep at the switch."

He didn't smile at her weak joke, and she wiped at the tears that were falling again. "I'm so sorry, Jack. I didn't mean for this to happen."

He sat heavily on the small stone bench and ran his fingers through his hair. "I don't know what to say, Amelia."

She stared quietly at him. She'd hoped he would hug her and tell her it was fine. She'd even allowed herself a small, sweet fantasy where Jack told her he loved her and was happy she carried his child.

He stared at her, his eyes dark with confusion and pain. "Amelia, I... I can't take you as my mate. You know that."

Only a few seconds ago, she was on the verge of sobbing, but now she could feel a thin thread of anger go through her. She welcomed it, opened her arms wide and embraced it. It was easier to deal with the anger than the sorrow.

"Yes, I know, Jack. You've made that perfectly clear."

He winced at her tone. "Amelia -"

"Don't," she said. "I didn't tell you about being pregnant because I want or expect something from you. I told you because you have the right to know. Now that you do, I'll be leaving."

"Leaving? What do you mean?" He stood up, and she backed away.

"I mean, I'm leaving. I can't stay here forever. You and your family have already been more than generous."

"You're not going back home," he said. "David will still be looking for you."

"Yes, I know," she snapped. "Don't worry about me. I'll figure something out."

"You're carrying my pup, Amelia. I won't allow you to leave," he said.

"Allow me?" She raised her eyebrows at him. "I hate to tell you this, Jack, but I'm a grown woman, and I'll do whatever I want. As you're so fond of reminding me, I am not your mate. You have no right to tell me what I can and cannot do."

"Jesus Christ, Amelia!" he shouted. "My pup grows in your belly."

"You won't be my mate, but I'm expected to stay with you as what – the whore who bears your pups?" she asked.

"Stop it. That isn't what I'm saying."

"I'm giving it up for adoption," she said.

"Like hell you are!" he roared.

"Jack, use your head. The odds of me being immune to the baby are slim. I won't be able to touch it, hold it, or kiss it. What kind of life is that for a child? What kind of life is that for me? To have a baby that I can never hold without some kind of barrier between us? You'd put me... you'd put your *child* through that?"

"Humans will adopt it," he said. "What happens when it shifts for the first time?"

"You and I both know that this child will most likely be unable to shift. I don't think that'll be a concern."

"*You* don't think it'll be a concern? Oh great, that makes me feel much better," he said.

She didn't reply, and he glared at her. "Fine. If you want to abandon our pup, I'll raise it alone."

Hurt and shock washed over her at his cruelty. She staggered back. "I'm not abandoning it. I'm just... you're such an asshole."

"Amelia, I'm sorry." His face was pale, and he looked sick to his stomach. He reached for her, and she stumbled towards the house on legs that felt like they might fold under her.

"Don't touch me," she said

"I didn't mean that, Amelia. I shouldn't have said it, and I'm sorry," he said.

She nodded woodenly, filled with sudden bone-deep weariness. "I know, Jack. Apology accepted."

"Where are you going?" he asked as she turned away.

"To bed. I'm tired, and I have a lot to think about."

"Please don't leave my parents' home, Amelia," he said. "Not until we talk more about this."

"I won't," she said.

"Do you promise?"

"Yes." She looked over her shoulder at him. "Will you give me some space tonight, Jack? I can sleep on the couch."

"You can have the bedroom. I won't bother you."

"Thank you." Her stomach churning, Amelia walked away.

* * *

"MOM, WHAT ARE YOU DOING HERE?" JACK STARED AT JOY AS she sat on the corner of his desk. He glanced around the busy precinct. "Is Amelia okay?"

"She's fine. Your brother asked me to stop by."

"What? Why?"

"Because you're being an idiot, that's why," Hank grumbled behind them as he joined them from his desk.

"I know Amelia's pregnant," Joy said.

Jack glared at Hank. "I told you that in confidence, Hank."

After spending a sleepless night on the couch, Jack had risen early and left for work without speaking to Amelia. When Hank arrived at work a couple of hours later, he'd immediately cornered Jack and demanded to know what was happening. Joy had called him at Sharon's and asked him to talk to Jack. Apparently, Amelia had been quiet and withdrawn at breakfast and wouldn't tell any of them what was wrong.

Miserable and worried about Amelia, Jack told Hank everything. Hank was sympathetic but, as far as Jack was concerned, not helpful. He'd simply told him that everyone knew Jack loved Amelia, and he needed to tell her that and ask her to be his mate.

He had brushed aside Jack's protests that it wasn't that simple and clapped him on the back. "She carries your pup in her belly, and you love her, little brother. It is simple enough."

Now, Jack snorted with irritation and stood up from his desk. He led Hank and Joy into an empty office and shut the door. "You should have kept your big mouth shut, Hank."

"Stop yelling at your brother," Joy said. "I already knew she was pregnant, Jack. Her scent changed weeks ago."

"Mom," Jack hesitated, "I know you just want to help but -"

"Why do you refuse to make her your mate? She loves you," Joy said.

"Because I know how much it hurt my birth father to leave his pack, and I know how it hurts you still," Jack said.

"What are you talking about, Jack?" Joy said.

He could hear the astonishment in her voice, but he knew the real truth. "You love Dad, I know that, but don't try to deny that you miss being in a pack. You chose to leave your kind to marry a human, and a part of you regrets it. I won't do that to Amelia. Becoming my mate means she'll be an outcast from the humans. She loves me now, but years from now, she'll have regrets, and her love will fade."

"Jack Stephen Emerson!" His mother's anger was plastered all over her face. "Are you suggesting that I do not love your father? That I wish I'd chosen my pack over him?"

She glared at him when he stayed silent. "I love your father deeply, and there has never been a moment where I regretted my decision to leave my pack to marry him. Do I miss being a part of a pack? Of course, I do, and I can't help that. But it has not and will not change my love for your father. He is my mate, and I'll love him until the day I die."

He shook his head. "Amelia isn't -"

"Amelia is already an outcast with the humans. She isn't even a human. She's a paranormal like we are, and your argument for not making her your mate is ridiculous," Joy said.

Jack glanced at Hank for help, but his brother shrugged. "Like I said – you're an idiot."

"Honey, listen to me." Joy cupped his face and stared up at him. "Amelia is not a Lycan. She doesn't feel the same urge you do to be part of a pack, nor will she regret her decision to become your mate. She wants to be with you. Everyone can see that. You need to stop projecting your feelings of loss without a pack onto her."

"I don't - I'm not feeling any loss," he said.

"You do." She gave Hank a loving glance. "You both do, and my heart hurts for the both of you. It is my greatest wish, as well as your father's that you and your brother find your own pack to join. You may be half-breeds, but the Lycan blood runs thick in your veins. You have tried to live as part of the human world for too long. You cannot, my love. You are who you are, and it is pointless to deny that you need a pack as much as any Lycan does."

"Mom -"

"You're scared, Jack. You've spent your entire life shutting yourself off from the humans and the Lycans. Then Amelia came along, and you fell in love with her, and now you don't know what to do. You've been trapped between the human world and the Lycan world. Unable to find a Lycan mate and afraid to love a human because you know deep down inside that you will eventually leave their world and join the Lycans. You never suspected that you would meet someone who would be so willing to follow you no matter where you decide to go."

"It's not just that," Jack said. "Amelia is sure she won't be able to touch our pup. She thinks it would be best if she gave it up for adoption. She says it would be torture for her and the pup if she couldn't touch it. She's right."

Joy kissed his forehead. "My love, you must convince her there's still a chance. She's immune to you and may be immune to the pup in her belly. Neither of you can give up hope."

Joy stepped back and squeezed his hands. "Come on. It's time to go home, tell Amelia you love her, and ask her to be your mate. Everything else will fall into place after that."

When Jack continued to hesitate, Hank rolled his eyes. "Do it, ya idiot."

"I do love her, Mom," Jack said hoarsely. "I love her so much."

"Then go home and tell her that."

CHAPTER 24

"Amelia? Can I make you some lunch? You ate nothing at breakfast," Leah said.

Amelia shook her head. "No. I'm not hungry. I'm too nauseous to be hungry."

Leah sat beside her on the couch. "I know we don't know each other well, but if you'd like to talk, I'm a good listener."

Amelia smiled at her. "Thank you, Leah. I really appreciate that. I'm just – I'm not ready to talk about it yet. I'm sorry."

"Don't be." Leah squeezed her hand through the glove and stood. "But I'm here if you want to talk, okay?"

Amelia nodded as Eric and Anthony entered the room.

"Hello, gorgeous." Anthony wiggled his eyebrows at Leah before planting a soft kiss on her neck and smacking her lightly on the ass.

"Stop it," she chastised him gently as Eric made a gagging noise and walked to the window.

"God, I'm bored. What I wouldn't give to shift and go running right now. I miss the forest," he said.

Amelia winced. They were outcasts because of her, and she'd never told them how sorry she was. She cleared her throat, but her cell phone rang before she could apologize. She pulled it from her pocket, smiling a little at the name on the call display. She hit the answer button. "Hi, Mom. How are you? I was going to call you later today."

"Sweet Amelia. It is your mate, David. How I have missed you."

She stiffened, her face paling, as Leah gave her a curious look.

"Be a good girl and pretend it's dear mommy on the phone, or you can listen to her screams as I gut her like a fish. Do you understand me?" David said.

"I – I'm good, Mom. I miss you," Amelia said.

"Very good. Listen closely, my sweet pet. I'm at your parents' house. I love that picture of you and your brother Richard hanging in the hallway. You look so sweet and inno-cent. Perhaps my seed will grow a girl in your belly that looks just like you. That would please you, would it not?"

"No, I don't know when I'm coming home." Amelia could hear the nerves in her voice, and she forced herself to smile widely at Leah.

"I want you to come home to me, Amelia. You're meant to be my mate, and I won't be denied. You have until six this evening to join me in your parents' home. For every minute that you're late, I'll cut off one of your mother's fingers, and then I'll start on your father. Do you understand me?"

"Yes," Amelia said as adrenaline raced through her veins.

"Come alone. If I even smell the half-Lycan's scent in the wind, I'll kill your parents, and then I'll kill him. Do you have any questions?"

"No."

"Good. See you soon, my sweet Amelia."

"Okay, Mom. I love you too, and I'll talk to you soon." Amelia ended the call and slipped her phone into her pocket.

"Amelia? Is everything okay?" Leah asked.

"What? Oh yeah. Everything's fine. I'm just missing my mom a little. You know how it is," Amelia said.

"Are you sure that's all it is?"

"Yes. I think I'll lie down for a while. I'm exhausted." Amelia nodded to the three Lycans and left the room as the fear poked jagged holes into her stomach lining.

* * *

"GONE? WHAT DO YOU MEAN GONE?" JACK SANK ONTO THE couch and stared blankly at his father.

"I don't know what happened. She said she was going to lie down. Leah went to check on her, and she was gone. She snuck out of the house while we were in the backyard. She took my car and left. We think she's been gone maybe half an hour. We've tried her cell phone, but she isn't answering."

"She promised me she wouldn't leave." Jack stared at his hands as Joy sat beside him and put her arms around him.

"You'll find her, Jack."

"How?" he asked. "She wouldn't have gone home - she knows it's too dangerous. She could be anywhere now. I can't believe she's gone. She promised me."

"Jack?" Leah said. "I think she might have gone home."

He frowned at her. "Why would you think that?"

"Just before she went to lie down, she got a phone call from her mother. It was strange. She was very pale, and although she said all the right things, there was something off about her conversation with her."

"What do you mean off?" Hank pushed away from the wall.

"I don't know. It just didn't feel right to me. She acted so weirdly afterward. I think her mother said something to her that made her believe she needed to come home."

Hank glanced at Jack and then back to Leah. "Are you sure about this, Leah? Do you really believe that she went home?"

Leah nodded. "I do."

Anthony stepped behind her and put his arm around her waist. "Leah has good instincts. She can read people very well. If she thinks that Amelia has gone home, then she has."

"What do you think, brother? Do we go back to Amelia's hometown?" Hank said.

"Yes. It's not like we have any other options anyway. If she didn't go home, she's gone, and I'll never see her or our pup again."

* * *

DREAD IN HER BELLY AND SHAKING LIKE A LEAF, AMELIA climbed the steps of her childhood home. She opened the door and slipped inside. "Mom? Dad?"

There was no answer, and, holding back the urge to vomit, she walked down the hallway and into the living room. The curtains were drawn, and it was dim in the room, but she had no problem seeing her parents standing together near the fireplace.

"Mom!" She rushed forward but flinched back when they tried to hug her. She took their hands in her gloved ones. "Are you all right?"

There was a large, ugly bruise on her dad's cheek, and blood still seeped from a claw mark on his forearm.

"I'm so sorry, Amelia." Her mother started to cry. "He said if I didn't call you, he would kill your father. I'm so sorry."

"Don't cry. You did the right thing," Amelia said. "Where is he?"

"I'm right here, my sweet. Are you anxious to see me? Have you missed me as I have missed you?" David's deep voice crawled over her, and she whirled around to see him standing in the shadows.

He stepped forward into the light, and she couldn't hold in her whimper of dismay. He was the biggest man she'd ever seen, with hard muscles and thick hair covering his body. Three Lycans in their wolf forms slinked into the living room. They snarled softly at her before joining David.

"You're so beautiful," David said. "I knew you were, of course. I saw you in the leech's head, but the real thing is so much better."

He stepped toward her, and Amelia made herself stay where she was. She flinched and turned her head when he leaned over her and sniffed deeply.

"You smell like him." His nose wrinkled before he smiled at her. "It doesn't matter. We will mate, and then my scent will cover your fair skin, not his."

He reached out to trace her cheek, and she flinched back.

A soft smile played on his lips. "I suspect that with your gift, you do not enjoy the touch of others. You let him touch you. But you won't allow me, your mate, to touch you? I find that upsetting."

"You are not my mate," she said. "And he is immune to me."

A flicker of anger crossed his face before he smiled at her. "Take your gloves off, my sweet. Let's see if I am immune to you as well."

She hesitated, and David stared at one of the Lycans. It stalked towards her parents, growling softly under its breath.

"Okay," she said quickly. "Okay, I'm taking them off." She peeled off her gloves and stuffed them into her pockets.

Don't think about the baby. Whatever you do, don't think about the baby. What do you think David will do to you if he discovers you're carrying Jack's child?

Amelia froze, her fear not for herself but for the child she carried. She had only found out she was pregnant a day ago, but already she felt a fierce, overwhelming desire to protect her child no matter the cost.

Understanding washed over her like a tidal wave. Her baby was all that mattered, and if she managed to survive today, she'd never let anyone take her child from her.

David was still holding out his hands, and he grunted impatiently. "Come, girl. Take my hands."

Steeling herself, she closed her eyes and repeated Richard's name in her head until it was a loud banging drumbeat that shut everything else out. She held out her trembling hands, and David clasped them roughly.

Immediately, David's thoughts flooded into her. The moon, bright and bloated in the night sky, sang its intoxicating song to her, and she shuddered all over as Richard's name beat faintly in her head. She could feel David's madness. She could feel the way it buzzed and itched at his brain, and she tried to pull her hands away, suddenly afraid that his insanity would leech into her and turn her mad as well. He refused to let her go, and she screamed as gruesome images of the animals and other Lycans he had hunted and killed flashed through her head.

David released her hands and staggered back. He panted hard, and his large body trembled as Amelia opened her eyes and stared at him, tears sliding down her cheeks.

"My God," he said. "What a truly remarkable power you have. You loved your brother very much. Even now, years after his death, you yearn for him and wish he still lived. That's good. Your compassion and loyalty will make you an excellent mother to our pups."

He glanced at Amelia's parents. They stared at Amelia with identical looks of confusion, and he turned back to her. "Do your parents not know of your marvellous gift, my sweet?"

She shook her head, and he grinned at her parents. "Your child is extraordinary. I want you to know that I'll take good care of her. You don't need to worry."

Amelia pulled her gloves from her pocket and placed them back on her hands, smoothing them up her arms. David held one meaty hand out to her. "Come, my sweet. We must get you back to my home to prepare you for our wedding. We'll be mated tonight, and later, I will take you to my bed and show you how to please me."

Amelia shuddered. Holding his hands had been more horrible than she could have imagined. What would happen to her if she had sex with him? She would go mad.

No, you won't. If you go mad, what will happen to the baby? You have to be strong and do what it takes to keep your baby safe. That's all that matters now.

David scowled at her. "Let's go, Amelia."

He glanced at her parents when she didn't move. "If you come with me now, I'll spare your parents' lives. If you argue or balk, I'll kill them. Do you believe me?"

She nodded and looked over her shoulders at her parents. "I love you."

"Amelia, no." her mother moaned. Her father started forward and was driven back by the three snarling, snapping Lycans.

"Dad, don't," Amelia said. "Everything will be fine. Just remember that I love you."

She smoothed on her gloves, took David's hand, and allowed him to lead her out of the living room. He stopped in the hallway and stuck his head back into the room. He stared at the three Lycans standing in front of Amelia's parents. "Wait ten minutes and then kill them both."

"NO!" Amelia screamed and beat at his large chest with both hands.

Her flailing fists caught him hard on the jaw, and he growled before raising his fist and giving her a hard blow to the temple. Darkness descended.

CHAPTER 25

"Amelia! Are you here?" Jack, followed closely by Hank, ran into Amelia's childhood home without knocking. "Amelia? Answer me – are you here?" He ran down the hallway and stuck his head into the living room. Her parents stood frozen against the far wall. He ran into the room.

"Laura, I'm looking for Amelia. Have you -"

The low growling from his left made his hackles rise. He turned to see the Lycan slink from the shadows and leap at him. He threw his hands up, catching it around the scruff as it slammed into him and knocked him to the floor.

Hank snarled, and Lupe barked as the wolf crouched over Jack. The stink of its hot breath surrounded him, and it snapped viciously at his face, its large white teeth gleaming in the dim light.

As he strained to push it off, he heard a loud yelp and Hank's howl of triumph. Jack brought his legs up, shifting them under the wolf's belly and heaved the wolf over his head with a grunt of effort. The wolf slammed into the wall, and there was the sound of breaking glass as several frames fell from the wall and hit the floor.

Jack leaped to his feet and whirled around. The wolf had staggered away from the wall, and Jack could feel the shift happening. Before he could shift, Anthony and Eric, in their wolf forms, bounded into the room and fell on the wolf. Amelia's mother screamed as they tore its throat open, and blood gushed from its neck. It made a gurgling whimper and died.

Hank howled again, and Amelia's parents cringed and covered their ears. The Lycan he had killed lay motionless against the wall, and the third wolf cowered in the corner, Lupe snarling and snapping at it. Anthony shifted and approached the frightened beast.

"Shift, Brian," he said. The wolf shifted with a soft whimper, and Jack stared at the young blonde man.

Brian fell to his knees. "I'm sorry, Anthony. I didn't want to do this, but David told us to kill them and – and we cannot disobey the alpha."

"David has gone crazy. He needs to be stopped." Anthony crouched beside the frightened Lycan and rested his hand on his shoulder. "You know I'm speaking the truth."

Brian wiped at his nose. "I know, Anthony."

"Can someone please tell me what's going on?" Laura moaned. Her face had gone completely white, and she shook so hard she could hardly stand. Her husband led her to a chair and sat her in it before running his hand through her hair.

"Shh, Laura. It's okay." He kissed her cheek and then stared at Jack. "Who are you? What are you?"

Before Jack could answer, Laura said, "He's Amelia's friend."

"I'm her mate," Jack said. "Has she been here?"

"Yes. He took her," Walter said. "He took our baby girl."

"When did they leave?" When Walter didn't reply, Jack reached out and shook him roughly. "When?"

"They left maybe fifteen minutes ago." Walter glanced at Brian, and Anthony still crouched in the corner. "Whatever they are, they were just about to kill us when they heard your car in the driveway."

Jack started for the door. Hank shifted back to his human form and grabbed his arm. "Jack, wait."

"Let me go! I need to find her. He's going to hurt her, Hank."

"We need a plan, little brother. The last time you confronted him, he almost killed you." Hank turned back to Amelia's parents. "What did the Lycan say?"

"Lycan?" Laura asked.

"The man who took Amelia - what did he say?" Hank said.

Laura glanced at Walter. "He said that she needed to go with him and prepare for their wedding and that they would be mated tonight."

Jack muttered a curse as Hank turned to Anthony. "Are you with us?"

Anthony nodded. "Yes. We'll help you stop David."

* * *

"You look very pretty." The young girl helping her dress was gentle and timid.

Amelia studied herself in the mirror. She wore a long, sheer white gown. It was an empire-style dress with a low neckline and long billowing sleeves. The bodice and the sleeves were silk and covered in lace, and the bodice clung to her full breasts. The silky material of the skirt brushed across her flat belly and down her legs.

The girl, she'd told Amelia her name was Tara, finished buttoning the row of white pearl buttons up the back of her dress. She went to gather Amelia's hair, and Amelia flinched away from her.

"Do not touch me," she said sharply.

The young girl made a frightened squeak. "I'm sorry."

"It's fine," Amelia said.

Tara was anxious around her, and Amelia couldn't understand why. "Why are you nervous?"

Tara swallowed hard, her face a little pale. "You are to be the alpha's mate. David would be angry with me if I upset or anger you. Have I upset you, ma'am?"

"No, and you should call me Amelia."

"Amelia." Tara smiled shyly at her as Amelia glanced around the large cabin. Her head ached miserably where David had hit her, and she was tired and cold, and the nausea was back with a vengeance. She rubbed her belly and took a few deep breaths.

"Whose cabin is this?"

"David's, and yours now, too."

"Tara, you know your alpha has gone crazy, right? He's brought me here against my will. I'm the mate of another." Amelia figured a small white lie wouldn't hurt. "I don't wish to marry David. Will you help me escape?"

"You belong to another?" Tara frowned.

"Yes," Amelia said quickly. "David took me from him. My mate should be given the right to fight for me."

She held her breath, hoping fervently that the young girl would help her. Leah had told her that male Lycans would occasionally lust after the same female. It was the tradition that the males fight for the right to the female's hand in marriage. Regardless of whether she favoured one male over the other, the woman would be automatically given to the winner as his mate.

Amelia had been horrified by that and unable to hide it from Leah.

"I know it's barbaric, but it rarely happens anymore," Leah had assured her. "And if it does, it's totally for show and meaningless. Even if the undesirable male wins, the female can reject his marriage proposal. Lycans believe it makes for more harmonious packs if their females are happy."

Now, Amelia gave Tara a pleading look. "Will you help me, Tara?"

Tara hesitated. "I'm sorry, I can't. If David finds out I helped you escape, he'll kill me."

Amelia blinked back the tears, and Tara said, "I'm sorry, Amelia. Please don't hate me."

"I don't." Amelia rested her hand against her belly again and stared at herself in the mirror.

She would be married to David tonight, and it was up to her to figure out a way to escape. Jack didn't know where she was. Even if he did, she wasn't sure he cared anyway.

He cares. He cares because you carry his child. He may not want you, but he wants the baby. He'll come looking for you.

She wiped away the hot tears sliding down her cheeks. It didn't matter. He wouldn't arrive in time to save her from David. She was on her own. She turned to Tara and smiled again at her. "I'm feeling hungry now, Tara. I think I'll go to the kitchen."

The young girl tried to follow her, and Amelia held up her hand. "I can find my way. Please, will you take my clothes to the bedroom?" Her purse, with her cell phone tucked into it, was missing, but she gathered up her jeans and t-shirt and handed them to Tara.

Tara hesitated, and Amelia said, "Tara, will I have to tell David that you weren't helpful to me?"

Tara shook her head. "No, but don't try to escape, Amelia. Don and Robert stand guard. Besides, there is nothing but forest for miles. You'll die of exposure if you leave."

Amelia nodded. "I'm not going to try to escape. I just want food to settle my stomach and some time to myself."

She walked toward the kitchen, praying that Tara didn't follow her. When Tara turned left down the hall and headed for the bedroom, Amelia sprinted into the kitchen. She started quietly opening the drawers. She quickly found a large butcher knife, but finding something to secure it to her arm was more difficult. Worried that Tara would return before carrying out her plan, she could have cried with relief when she opened a drawer with batteries, old receipts, and a jumble of elastic bands.

She pushed up her dress sleeve and placed the knife against the inside of her forearm before using the rubber bands to secure the blade to her arm. She moved her arm experimentally, and one of the rubber bands split as the knife's sharp edge sliced it apart.

"Shit," she muttered. She secured another few rubber bands to the knife. She would have to be careful not to move her arm very much. She had left the handle free, and when the right moment came, she would grab the handle, twist the knife so the blade cut through the bands and then plunge the knife into David.

"Easy," she whispered, pushing her sleeve down. The billowy material hid the knife nicely, and she moved to the fridge as she heard Tara's footsteps in the hall. The thought of killing another living being, even someone like David, made Amelia feel like vomiting, but she pushed away her apprehension. She would do whatever it took to keep her baby safe.

CHAPTER 26

"How lovely you are." David's eyes swept down her body; his gaze lingered on her breasts, and his nostrils flared as he inhaled deeply.

"You will make a lovely mate," he said. "And our children will be powerful Lycans. All other Lycans will bow before them. Come, Amelia."

With Tara following her, Amelia trailed after David. He led her toward the clearing where the rest of the pack had gathered in a circle. He stopped in the middle of the circle and smiled at the other Lycans. "Today marks a new era for us. Today, I take a human woman as my mate. But she is no ordinary human, and the pups that she will bear for me will bring me – us- unimaginable power."

He turned and smiled at Amelia. "Come, my sweet. Stand by my side, and we will begin the ceremony that will unite us."

She took a tentative step forward and then another. Her heart raced, and her palms were sweating, and she wanted to grab the knife from her arm and stab David in the face with it. She made herself relax. The time to use the blade would be later when they were alone in his bed.

"Come." He gestured at her impatiently. "Don't make me -"

"David!"

David's eyes narrowed. Amelia's heart tripped into over-time when she saw Anthony, Eric, and a man she didn't recognize emerge from the trees surrounding the clearing.

"What are you doing, David?" Anthony asked.

"So, the traitors return," David snarled. "Where is your mate? I would not want her to miss it when I rip your head from your body."

He started forward, and Anthony turned to the Lycans gathered around David and Amelia. "Brothers and sisters, this woman belongs to another! She is a Lycan's mate, and David has stolen her like a coward in the night."

There was a collective gasp, and David hesitated as the pack members stared at him.

"He lies!" David finally shouted. "You would believe a traitor over your alpha?"

"He isn't lying," Eric said. "He instructed me to kidnap the woman weeks ago. When I tried, her mate saved her."

Anthony studied the pack. "Some of you were there in the forest. You heard the Lycan and David speak, and -"

"He is not her mate!" David bellowed. Amelia cringed at the rage in his voice.

"He is," Anthony said calmly. "David ordered you to kill the Lycan in the forest because he desired Jack's mate. David is mad. Do you not see that?"

"Kill them," David said.

The pack hesitated, and David glared at them. "Kill the traitors! They spread lies about your alpha! This woman has no mate. The Lycan may have been interested in her before, but he is no longer. He has abandoned her. She returned to her home willingly without him."

"She carries his pup in her belly," Anthony said.

David staggered back. "You lie."

"He doesn't," Amelia said in the sudden silence. She turned and grabbed Tara's hand, pushing the memory of Leah telling her she was pregnant and the memory of the positive pregnancy test into the front of her mind.

Tara cried out, and Amelia moaned quietly as the moon filled her head. For a moment, she was Tara in wolf form, running through the trees, panting and chasing after her mother and feeling an indescribable joy at the brief glimpses of the moon between the trees.

Tara tore free of her grip and stared mutely at Amelia, her mouth open and lips trembling. "It's true," she said. "I - I could see it in her head."

David howled angrily, and the pack members backed away a few feet. He clenched his fists and howled again, pointing his face to the sky as his bones cracked and fur grew on his face.

"David!" Anthony shouted. The giant Lycan turned towards him, his eyes glowing and his face hidden behind the thick layer of fur. "You can't take her as your mate."

David laughed. "Where is her mate? He sends you to rescue her? If he loves her, why does he not come himself?"

Jack and Hank stepped out of the trees and joined Anthony and the others. Lupe followed closely behind them.

David snarled at them and turned to the others. "Kill him! Now!"

When they didn't move, he howled in frustration and anger. Jack stepped into the circle and approached David. Amelia stared at him, her heart swelling with love at the sight of his familiar face. He glanced briefly at her, his eyes warm and calm, and she stepped toward him.

David immediately growled at her. "Stay where you are."

"I challenge you," Jack said.

David hesitated, and Anthony joined the circle. "He has issued a challenge, David. You must accept it or hand over the woman so she can rejoin her mate."

"She is mine!" David shouted. "Kill him!"

He stared at his pack. Although they looked away, and some even whimpered, no one moved.

"Jack," Amelia said.

He smiled at her. "I love you, Amelia. You are my mate."

"I love you too." She couldn't stop the tears as Jack turned to David.

"Do you accept my challenge, or will you show the pack your true cowardly nature?" Jack asked.

"I will rip off your head and bathe in your blood!" David roared. "She will watch you suffer as no other Lycan has suffered!"

He shifted to his wolf form. Amelia stumbled backward, fresh fear washing over her. David was a giant of a wolf. His paws were larger than her head, and when he rose onto his back feet and howled, he towered over Jack. His pack howled in reply, some shifting while others paced restlessly back and forth as they watched Jack shift.

Jack was a large wolf, but he looked small compared to David, and Amelia was suddenly certain Jack would die.

As Jack and David trotted toward each other, Hank and Lupe circled them and joined Amelia. She stared up at Hank, her voice shaky. "We have to help him, Hank."

"We can't, Amelia," Hank said as Lupe licked Amelia's hand.

"David is too big, too powerful. He'll kill him," she said.

"Don't count Jack out just yet," Hank said as the two wolves circled each other, panting and grinning.

She could barely hold in her scream when the two wolves

leaped at each other. They met in the air, their bodies crashing into each other before dropping to the ground. They rolled around, their bodies twisting and turning and growls and snarls tearing from their throats.

It was almost impossible to tell who was winning. Her breath coming in short gasps and her hands gripping her dress in tight fists, Amelia watched in horrified silence as the Lycans fought viciously for long minutes. She couldn't stop her loud cry when David pinned Jack to the ground. Before he could rip out his throat, Jack bit his leg, his sharp teeth sinking to the bone, and David howled with pain before leaping off of him.

Jack staggered to his feet as David backed away. Grinning savagely, saliva dripping out of his mouth, Jack leaped for him as David returned to his human form. With an angry roar, David grabbed Jack by the scruff of his neck and hurled him into the trees.

"No!" Amelia screamed when Jack slammed into a tree. He fell to the ground, shifting back to his human form as he fell. He slumped forward, blood streaming from his head and was still.

"Jack!" Amelia cried. She ran after Hank and Lupe as they raced toward Jack's body.

David reached out and snagged her dress, yanking her toward him. His eyes were still green, and his teeth jutted between his lips. They had cut into his lips, and blood flowed freely down his chin.

"You're mine now." He grinned at her, his teeth red with blood as he wrapped one arm around her waist. "I've killed your mate, and I'll kill his pup in your belly," he said as he yanked her towards him. "You'll never -"

He grunted quietly in surprise before he pushed away from Amelia and stared down at his naked torso.

The butcher knife was embedded deep in his side, and he

233

touched the handle before returning his gaze to Amelia's face. Her smile of triumph faded when he grinned and yanked the knife from his flesh. Blood flowed steadily for a few seconds, and she watched in horror as it clotted and the wound began to close in front of her eyes.

"You have spirit. I will enjoy breaking it." David reached for her, his fingernails, sharp claws, and eyes glowing with madness. Amelia cringed back, and David laughed. "You can't kill me, little girl. No one can."

"I can," Jack's voice was quiet but perfectly understandable.

David grunted and fell to his knees, his hand reaching behind him to touch his back. Blood flowed, and he stared at his fingers as Amelia stared at Jack standing behind David. Blood covered his right hand, where the fingernails were long and sharp. Before David could climb to his feet, Jack gripped David's long hair and yanked the Lycan's head back. Before he buried his face in David's throat, Amelia had a brief glimpse of Jack's face, half-Lycan and half-human.

David whimpered, a sound of surprise more than pain before his body stiffened, and he shuddered once. Jack released him and stepped back, staring in satisfaction as the blood gushed from David's torn throat and down his chest. He touched the flood of warmth on his chest, stared at the blood on his fingers, and pitched face forward into the dirt.

Goosebumps rose on Amelia's flesh when Jack, his face covered in blood, raised his face to the night sky and howled. The pack of Lycans dropped to their knees, and when Jack howled again, they answered his call.

* * *

SEVEN MONTHS LATER

. . .

"How is she?" Joy hurried down the hospital corridor and grabbed Jack's arm.

"She's tired. It was a hard labour, and the babies ended up tangled in each other's cords. They had to do a C-section."

"What did she have?" Joy asked.

Jack grinned. "A boy and a girl."

"That's so wonderful! Tom and Hank are on the way, but I know the pack wants to know too."

She pulled out her cell phone and then hesitated. "Can she touch them?"

"We don't know yet." Jack ignored the fear that was burrowing into his stomach. "She just came back from recovery. I'm looking for a nurse to ask her to bring the babies from the nursery."

Joy squeezed his arm. "She'll be able to touch them, I know it. She couldn't hear their thoughts in the womb. It has to mean she's immune to them."

"Maybe," Jack said, but he could hear the anxiety in his voice.

"I'll find the nurse. You stay with your mate," Joy said.

Jack slipped into the hospital room and sank into the chair beside Amelia's bed. Amelia gave him a tired smile. "Did you find a nurse?"

"Mom is finding her."

"Okay."

"How do you feel?" He leaned over and kissed her.

"Sore. And I don't want to stay in the hospital." She shifted a little in the bed.

"It'll only be for a day or two, and then we will be back with the pack, and you'll have plenty of hands to help you with the babies."

Amelia smiled at him, her eyes drifting shut.

Jack sat back in his chair. The last seven months had brought a lot of change to his and Amelia's lives. Good change, but that didn't mean they weren't both still adjusting. His defeat of David meant he'd become the alpha of the pack. He'd quit his job and moved to Amelia's small town. He hadn't expected to keep working as a cop, but Ray immediately offered him a job.

Three months later, he and Amelia were married, and they and the entire pack had moved to a quiet neighbourhood on the outskirts of town. Two months later, Hank, Sharon, Tom, and Joy joined them.

"Did you let Ray know I had the babies?" Amelia asked without opening her eyes.

"I did."

"I feel bad for ruining his retirement party," she said.

Jack laughed. "It wasn't your fault you went into labour. Besides, he keeps saying he's retired - hell, he's even handed over his office to me – but he's at the department today. Helping out, he says, while I'm busy with the new babies."

"Have you seen them?" she asked.

"Yes." He smiled at her when she opened her eyes. "They're beautiful. They look just like their mother."

Her return smile was pale, and he could smell her anxiety and her fear. "Jack, what if I can't -"

"You will," he said. "I know it."

The door opened, and a nurse entered, followed by Joy. They were each holding a baby, and Jack was confident he heard the pounding of Amelia's heart as he used the button to raise the bed into a sitting position.

The nurse handed Jack his son and left the room as Joy circled the bed. She smiled at Amelia. "Are you ready, sweetheart?"

Amelia nodded as Jack said with a confidence he didn't quite feel. "It'll be fine, Amelia. You'll see."

Joy and Jack placed her babies on her blanket-covered lap. They stepped back as Amelia stared down at the tiny faces. Her hands shaking, she reached out and rested her fingers on their soft cheeks.

Jack's heart sank when she stiffened, and her mouth trembled. Tears slipped down her cheeks as she stared at her babies and slowly moved her hands away.

"I'm so sorry, honey." He reached for the baby closest to him. "We'll make it work. I promise you."

Amelia knocked his hands away and looked up at him. Her face was wet with tears, but she smiled hugely at him, and his love for her nearly overwhelmed him.

"I can't feel them. Either of them!" She started to sob, and he sat on the side of the bed, putting his arm around her thin shoulders.

"Honey, are you – are you sure?"

"Yes! Yes! I can't feel them." She picked up their daughter and pressed her lips to her forehead before setting her down carefully and doing the same to their son. "Jack – they're blank to me."

Jack hugged her hard. "I love you, Amelia."

"I love you too, Jack."

EPILOGUE

"Mom! Tell him to quit bugging me!"

Amelia twisted in her seat and stared at her children in the back seat of the SUV. "Honestly, Ian. You're sixteen years old. Stop teasing your sister."

"She started it," Ian muttered. His face darkened into a stubborn scowl, and he looked so much like his father that Amelia could barely keep the smile from her face.

"You have to use your head, Ian." Jack stared gravely at him in the rear-view mirror. "Don't let your emotions rule you."

"Now you sound like Grandpa Tom," Ian snorted.

Amelia grinned. "We're almost to your grandparents. Can you and your sister please try to be civil to each other until then?"

"Will Grandma Joanna be there?" Emily asked.

Amelia didn't answer. Jack was rubbing her thigh slowly, and his big hand was sending all sorts of delicious shivers down her spine. She gave him a warm and inviting smile, and he winked at her.

"Mom?"

"Hmm?"

"Will Grandma Jo be there?" Emily asked.

Amelia nodded. "Yes. Grandma Laura invited her to have supper with us tonight."

"Good. I want to show her my latest drawing." Emily, her dark hair spilling over her shoulders, handed her mother a piece of paper.

"It's beautiful, honey." Amelia smiled at her and handed back the piece of paper. She winced as the sharp edge of the paper slipped across the pad of her finger.

"What happened?" Jack asked.

"Just a paper cut."

"Let me see." Emily held out her hand, and Amelia reached back so she could look at her finger. There was a tingling, a brief feeling of warmth, and the sting of the paper cut was gone. Amelia examined the now smooth pad of her finger.

"Thank you, honey."

"You're welcome, Mama." Emily grinned.

"You're welcome, Mama," Ian parroted, and Emily punched him hard on the shoulder.

"Shut up, Ian!"

"You shut up!"

"You're just jealous because I have a gift, and you don't."

A low growling erupted from Ian's chest, and his eyes glowed green. The wispy hair on his chin and upper lip thickened.

"Ian Richard Emerson. Control yourself," Amelia warned.

Emily rolled her eyes. "He does that all the time. He's even been doing it at school. He thinks Sara Ferguson will date him if he has actual hair on his face."

"Shut up, Emily! You're no better than me. You keep

turning your eyes green just because you think Mark will notice you more than when you have your boring old brown eyes." Ian curled his lip up at her.

She stuck out her tongue, her own eyes glowing green briefly. "Whatever, Ian."

She giggled when the large canine sitting in the cargo section of the SUV leaned over the back seat and swiped her cheek with his tongue.

"Cut it out, Charlie." She rubbed Charlie's cheek affectionately before pushing him gently away.

Charlie, the second-generation offspring of Lupe and Luna, panted happily before nudging Ian with his cold nose. The boy didn't respond. His usually tanned face had gone pale, and he was chewing on one nail.

"Dad?" he said hoarsely.

"Yeah?" Jack glanced in the rearview mirror and frowned. "Ian? What's wrong?"

"I think you should pull over."

"What?"

"Please pull over. Something – something's wrong." The boy was nearly begging now, and Amelia, alarm tugging at her nervous system, turned to Jack.

"Pull over, Jack."

They were climbing a small but steep hill. Jack pulled the SUV to the side of the road just before they reached the top of the hill and put it in park.

"Ian? Are you okay?" Both he and Amelia turned to stare at him.

"I don't know. I just feel weird. I have a horrible feeling like -"

Emily gasped loudly. Two sports cars, the sun winking off their windshields, crested the top of the hill. They were drag racing, their vehicles taking up both lanes and as they roared by the SUV parked on the side of the road, Charlie barked piercingly out the window.

"Charlie, enough!" Jack said. He stared in disbelief at Amelia.

She studied Ian. "Ian, honey? Did you know that was going to happen?"

I knew something was going to happen. I don't know how, but I just knew. Do you believe me?"

Amelia nodded. "Of course we do, sweetie."

She reached out and squeezed his hand. "We'll talk to Grandma Joanna at dinner, but I think you've just discovered your gift."

Jack pulled out onto the road again, and they continued driving silently. After a few moments, Jack squeezed her thigh, and she stared at him.

"Are you okay?" he asked quietly.

"Yes. I think he has the same gift as Richard. Right before the car accident, Richard tried to warn me, but I didn't listen. I should have listened to him."

"You didn't know." He squeezed her leg again. "You do now, and it just helped save our lives."

"Yes." She gave him a shaky smile as he pulled into Laura and Walter's driveway and shut off the engine.

She unclicked her seatbelt and slid across the seat, tangling her hands in Jack's hair and kissing him deeply. He returned her kiss, his hands sliding around her to pull her against his broad chest.

"Oh gross," Ian groaned from the back seat.

"Blecch." Emily rolled her eyes, and the twins quickly escaped the vehicle with Charlie on their heels.

Laura, Walter, and Joanna were walking out of the house, and Amelia smiled against Jack's mouth when Ian yelled, "Grandma Jo! Guess what?"

Jack leaned back and pushed a strand of her long dark hair back from her face. "I love you, honey."

Amelia smiled and pressed her mouth briefly against his. "I love you too, Jack."

Want more Lycan goodness? Keep reading for an excerpt from Elizabeth's novel, "The Recruit, Book One."

Hannah peered into the hallway. It was empty, and she crept silently through the maze of hallways until she arrived at one of the training rooms. She eased the door open, moving confidently across the room in the dark. She reached up, grabbed the metal bar above her head, and pulled herself up with a grunt of effort. Her already tired and strained arm muscles screamed at her, but she fixed Sara's sweet face in the front of her mind and continued to haul her body up and down.

After a few minutes, she let her body drop to the floor. She was panting harshly, her arms shaking and burning, but she had done nearly fifteen pull-ups – her best effort yet. She gave herself five minutes to rest, lying on her back on the soft mat and staring blindly at the ceiling as she shook out her arms.

She forced herself to stand and move to the far side of the gym. She knew from past experience that if she waited much longer, her body would seize up, and the rest of her exercises would be brutally painful. There was a heavy bag hanging from the ceiling, and, using touch only, she located a pair of gloves and fumbled into them.

She'd been in the program for five weeks now, and for the last two weeks, when the rest of the recruits had tumbled exhausted into their beds, she would sneak out of the dormitories and return to the gym. She forced herself to run laps, lift weights, and practice pull-ups and push-ups. Afraid of being caught, she did all of it in total darkness. The first few nights, she had tripped over exercise machines, stubbed nearly every toe on rows of weights, and once even ran face-first into a wall, but now it seemed her night vision was improving, and she could easily navigate in the blackness.

She punched the heavy bag, the vibrations running back through her arms and into her aching shoulders and back. She ignored the pain. Even with her extra work at night, she was barely keeping up with the other recruits, and she knew that Will was dangerously close to kicking her out of the program. She could see it every time he looked at her.

It wasn't just physical exhaustion, either. When the recruits weren't training, they were in classes with Isabelle. Isabelle was in her thirties with long blonde hair and a slender body. She was gorgeous. Her eyes were an impossible shade of blue, and she had the softest-looking skin Hannah had ever seen. Over the last few weeks, she taught them the history of the vampires and, to a limited degree, other paranormal creatures.

Hannah could still remember the day Will joined them for one of their classes, sitting quietly in the back as they discussed the various weapons used against vampires over the years. Alison and Frank were in a heated debate over whether make-shift weapons from household items would be useful in a pinch when Will snorted loudly and stood.

"If you find yourself weaponless around vampires, your greatest chance for survival is to run." He looked at each of them, his gaze landing on Hannah's face last. "You run, and you hide."

She shook her head, wiping his face from her mind, and concentrated on hitting the bag with firm, hard punches like Mannie taught her. She snatched gulps of air into her burning lungs. She wanted to quit and go back to her bed in the dormitory. She wanted to soak her pillow with the tears that were always so close to the surface, but she thought of Sara.

She thought about Sara's tenth birthday and how excited she was when her parents had rented out the movie theatre for her and her friends. She thought about the first night that Sara had come home drunk. Hannah had squirrelled her away to the bathroom before their parents could see her. She held Sara's hair back as she threw up wretchedly, vowing breathlessly between each bout of vomiting that she would never drink again.

Memory after memory of Sara flooded her mind, and she punched the bag in front of her harder and harder. Her breath was coming in short, shallow gasps and tears mixed freely with the sweat dripping down her face. So engrossed was she in her memories and the rhythmic thumping noise of her gloved hands that when a hard hand fell onto her shoulder, she screamed and turned, punching wildly at the huge shadow behind her.

* * *

Will cursed as one of Hannah's gloves caught him on the chin. She had screamed only once before falling silent. As he wrapped an arm around her waist, she writhed and squirmed like a wild cat, panting harshly and pounding his back with her gloved fists.

"Hannah, stop!" he said as her foot connected solidly with

his knee. He yelped like a wounded puppy, stepped backward, and tripped over his feet. He fell onto his back, dragging Hannah down with him.

She headbutted him in the chin, and he just managed to protect his balls from her knee before she landed a blow to his stomach.

"Enough!" he roared and flipped her onto her back, covering her struggling body with his own and pinning her arms above her head.

"It's Will!" he spoke into her ear as she panted and wiggled under him.

Her body froze, and then she sagged against the floor. "Will?"

"Yes."

"You scared the hell out of me!"

"What are you doing in here?" he asked.

"Nothing," she muttered.

"Don't lie to me," he warned.

"I'm just – just practicing, okay? I'm not breaking any rules."

"Actually," he said, "there is a rule about leaving the dormitory after lights out. You know that."

"I highly doubt that going to the gym after lights out is what they meant by breaking the rules," she scoffed. She tried to heave him off of her, but he settled his weight more firmly against her.

"I would think you get enough physical activity during the day. If you're looking for night activities, I can think of something entirely more pleasant for you to participate in." He said the last sentence in a low whisper, and her curvy body shivered against his

"Could you get off me, Will? You're too heavy," she said.

Will had excellent night vision, and he studied her face. Her dark eyes were huge, and despite her steady tone, he could see her lips trembling, and her entire body was shaking under his. He took a deep breath. He could smell the sharp tang of her sweat and the scent of strawberries under that. She must eat a lot of strawberries. The scent almost always lingered on her.

"Will?" she prompted and pulled against his hands holding her arms captive.

"Why are you practicing at night?" He tugged the gloves from her hands, tossing them to the side before propping himself up on his elbows above her but keeping her pinned to the floor with his lower body.

She flexed her fingers experimentally and then pushed at his chest. He refused to move, and she sighed in frustration.

"Tell me," he said.

* * *

She didn't want to tell him, but lying in the dark, his hard body on top of hers and feeling way too… right, she didn't have much choice. "Because I need to get better. Because I'm not stupid, and I know you're this close to kicking me out of the program. Because every time I close my eyes at night, all I see is Sara's face."

To her horror, she could feel tears dripping down her cheeks. The last thing she wanted to do was cry in front of Will. He already thought she was pathetic enough.

To her surprise, he roughly wiped away her tears with his thumbs. "It gets better."

"Does it?" she said. "I don't think it does."

"I promise it does."

She could just make out his features in the dark. "Who did you lose?"

"My father, my mother," he paused, "my brother and sister. They attacked us in our beds while we slept. I was still young, just a small child, and I had a nightmare. My mother was in my room when they broke in. She hid me in the closet before they drained her."

"I'm so sorry, Will," she whispered. Even in the darkness, she could see the pain in his eyes, and it started a strange twisting in her stomach. She lifted her head and pressed her lips against his without thinking about it.

He froze and then pulled away, sitting up and staring silently at her. She blushed and pushed herself into a sitting position, ignoring how her muscles screamed at her.

"Oh God, I'm sorry. I shouldn't have done that," she said.

He didn't reply. With a groan of embarrassment, she struggled to stand, praying he wasn't about to kick her out of the program. Before she could gain her feet, he reached out and yanked her into his lap. He cupped the back of her head and kissed her hungrily.

* * *

ABOUT THE AUTHOR

Elizabeth Kelly was born and raised in Ontario, Canada. She moved west as a teenager and now lives in Alberta with her husband and a menagerie of pets. She firmly believes that a person can survive solely on sushi and coffee, and only her husband's mad cooking skills prevents her from proving that theory.

For more information about Elizabeth, check out her website at

www.elizabethkelly.ca

facebook.com/EKellyBooks
instagram.com/elizabethkelly_author
amazon.com/Elizabeth-Kelly/e/B00EOHZ0MS
bookbub.com/authors/elizabeth-kelly

ALSO BY ELIZABETH KELLY

Tempted Series

Tempted

Twice Tempted

Forever Tempted

Breathless

Tempted Trilogy (Books 1-3)

Red Moon Series

Red Moon

Red Moon Rising

Dark Moon

Alpha Moon

Pale Moon

The Recruit Series

The Recruit (Book One)

The Recruit (Book Two)

The Recruit (Book Three)

The Recruit (Book Four)

The Recruit (Book Five)

The Recruit (Book Six)

The Shifters Series

Willow and the Wolf (Book One)

Ava and the Bear (Book Two)

Katarina and the Bird (Book Three)

Porter's Mate (Book Four)

Bria and the Tiger (Book Five)

Rosalie Undone (Book Six)

The Dragon's Mate (Book Seven)

Rise of the Jaguar (Book Eight)

The Assassin and the Bear (Book Nine)

Elora and the Crow (Book Ten)

The Draax Series

Reign (Book One)

Rule (Book Two)

Rebel (Book Three)

Surrender (Book Four)

Survive (Book Five)

Salvation (Book Six)

Harmony Falls Series

Sweet Harmony (Book One)

Perfect Harmony (Book Two)

Forbidden Harmony (Book Three)

Redeeming Harmony (Book Four)

Absolute Harmony (Novella)

Beautiful Harmony (Book Five)

Reckless Harmony (Book Six)

Seasoned Romance Series

Bet Your Heart on Me (Book One)

Take a Chance on Me (Book Two)

Place Your Trust in Me (Book Three)

Individual Books

The Necessary Engagement

Amelia's Touch

The Rancher's Daughter

Healing Gabriel

The Contract

A Home for Lily

Saving Charlotte

Shameless

The Fairy Tales Collection

Broken

An Unlikely Seduction

Holiday Romance

The Christmas Wife

The Christmas Rescue

The Christmas Nanny

The Christmas Boss

Sordid Games